MY SCORNED BEST FRIEND

PIPER RAYNE

Cover Design: By Hang Le

Cover Photo: Wander Aguiar Photography

1st Line Editor: Joy Editing

2nd Line Editor: My Brother's Editor

Proofreader: My Brother's Editor

About My Scorned Best Friend

Xavier and Clara kissing in a tree...

When your best friend growing up is a girl, that's the song your classmates taunt you with over and over again. But it was never like that... until now.

It's always been Clara and me. She's the only one who truly knows me. After I was drafted into the NFL and ended up the starting quarterback for the San Francisco Kingsmen, I begged her to come with me. But she had her own life and responsibilities back in our small Alaskan town, so I didn't fault her for staying.

We remained the best of friends despite the distance. I'd hang with her in Alaska during the off season, and she'd visit me in California while I was playing. Then, one night the lines blurred for the briefest of moments and set in motion a series of events that changed everything.

I'm not proud of the decisions I made after that fateful night, and I plan on making amends, because I need Clara back in my life. But not as my best friend—as my everything.

my scorned best FRIEND

The Greenes

Hank's Kids

Cade Greene (35)
Co-owner Truth or Dare Brewery
Fisher Greene (33)
Sheriff
Xavier Greene (31)
Pro Football Player
Adam Greene (29)
Forest Ranger
Chevelle Greene (28)
Water Boat Tourist

Marla's Kids

Jed Greene (35)
Co-owner of Truth or Dare Brewery
Nikki Greene (32)
Radio Host
Mandi Greene (30)
Owner of SunBay Inn
Posey Greene (26)
Owner of Fringe

Hank and Marla's Kid

Rylan Greene (15)

Chapter One

Xavier

I never thought that when I finally got everything I'd ever dreamed of, I'd be this fucking miserable.

My entire life, I've gone with my gut. I trust my decisions —both on and off the field. I'm one of those one-in-a-million cases. I left my small town with a scholarship to a DI college to play football, entered the draft and was a first-round pick, then two years ago, I signed a five-year contract that's still the biggest in the league.

I don't say all that with arrogance. The fact that I have a horseshoe up my ass isn't lost on me. Guys like me—from small schools in remote areas—don't get looked at by colleges. They sure as hell don't get as far as being the best quarterback in the league. But here I am. And despite all that, I'm unhappy.

My phone dings as I'm eating my breakfast before prac-tice, and I pick it up to see a DM from Sessilee. She's my ex's good friend, and ever since Giulia and I broke up, she's been popping up in my DMs.

Sessilee: *I'm in San Fran. How about dinner?*

I'm not exactly a mind reader when it comes to women,

but even I know that going to a dinner where Sessilee will one hundred percent snap a picture or tag me in some shit will stir up drama.

Me: *Sorry, Coach has me on a strict regimen. Next time for sure.*

The three dots appear immediately, which is probably meant to entice, but now that I have my phone in hand, I do what I've done every day for the last week—I scroll to my text messages and make sure I didn't miss a reply from Clara. Like every other time I've looked, the last text in the thread is my own.

Me: *You looked good tonight.*

Clara's my best friend, or my ex-best friend I suppose, but I could never think of her like that, even if she's not talking to me and our relationship has become strained to the degree of archrivals. She and my family got stuck on a layover last week after a family vacation in Hawaii that I couldn't take since it's my preseason. The minute I saw her, all I wanted to do was give her a hug and talk out our issues, put it all behind us, but I'm a coward. Instead, I waited until we'd parted that night and sent a message that should've said I'm sorry. But as always, I'm too fucking proud.

Messages from Sessilee trickle in as if the woman can't for the life of her form her thoughts in complete sentences. Instead, it's a string of two or three words per message.

I keep thumbing up as if miraculously, Clara will decide to forgive me. I tell myself the same bullshit I have every day —that Clara just returned from vacation and came home to a lot of work at the town library, which hasn't afforded her time to respond to my message yet.

After picking up my plate, I put it in the dishwasher and start the machine before I grab my bag and head out of my condo. On the elevator ride down, I scold myself for being in such a mindfuck.

I'm Xavier fucking Greene and I have the world at my fingertips. I can get into any restaurant in this town, even if it's the new hot place. Kids wear my jerseys. Hell, adults wear my jerseys. People stop me on the streets for pictures and autographs. I'm in sponsorship ads plastered across the glitziest cities in the country. This is what I've worked for my entire life. I should be fucking happy.

I'm so distracted by my thoughts that I don't realize at first that the elevator has stopped three floors below mine. My teammate, Ben Noughton, walks in, his head down and looking at his phone, a smile tipping up the corners of his lips. He's probably going to fill me in on last night's conquest.

He looks up and sees me. "X, what's up?"

"Morning." I press the door shut button to get this ride over with sooner. Which is absurd because Ben's been one of my best friends on the team ever since I started with the San Francisco Kingsmen.

"I never realized how funny Clara is," he says.

I tense and whip my head in his direction. He doesn't bother looking at me, his thumbs continuing to tap on the phone screen.

"I mean, at first I was all in because she's a librarian, you know."

Oh, I know, fucker.

"The whole sexy librarian with dark-framed glasses in a pair of black sheer stockings—"

"Keep in mind, she's my best friend."

Ben has no idea what went down with us.

"Funny you mention that." He glances at me. "I asked her why she hasn't been down here in the past two years."

My gut twists and I reposition my gym bag over my shoulder. I wait for him to continue.

"She said she didn't want to step on toes because of Giulia. That people might assume things because you're best friends."

Where did my truthful Clara disappear to?

Ben shrugs it off. "Anyway, I told her to come down when we play Seattle. With the rivalry between our teams, it'll make for one great party when we kick their ass."

My throat dries at the thought of Clara being here that weekend. The fact she'd be there because of Ben is another prick in my throat.

"And what did she say?" I do my best to keep my voice even.

He pockets his phone, his permanent smile still in place. "Said she'd think about it. She's kind of reserved, huh?"

The elevator stops on the bottom floor, and we step out, both saying good morning to our doorman, Kerbie. He opens the door and my car is there, waiting for me.

When Kerbie opens the car door, Ben slides in. "We're going to the same place, right?"

"Thank you," I say to Kerbie and follow Ben in.

What would've been an enjoyable ride by myself to the arena will now be filled with Ben's nonstop talk about Clara.

Sure enough, the second the door shuts, he turns and asks me, "What does she like to do for fun?"

I shrug, pretending I'm reading something on my phone, but all the words are melting together.

"Come on, X. I want to make it nice when she comes down. We can't talk about books, so help a brother out here."

"If, you mean?"

His forehead wrinkles. "What?"

"*If* she comes. She didn't say she was coming for sure."

"Hello, I'm Ben Noughton. I know I'm probably not her usual type, but—"

"What do you think her usual type is?" I've known Clara my entire life, and even I'm not sure I know her type.

"I'll bet she likes really smart dudes. Ones with a pipe and a plaid coat with the patches on the elbows."

A laugh escapes me despite how uncomfortable I am with this conversation. "And you think a lot of those guys live in Alaska?"

"Probably not. That's why she's still available. I mean, she's smokin' and now that she's a blonde... Damn, how could any guy not want her?"

"Yeah, right." I agree with Ben, because of course Clara would make any guy happy. Her only negative trait is that she's stubborn as hell, which is the reason we've yet to make up after our blowout.

"So? X?"

We pull up to the arena and I grab my bag, ready to flee this nightmare of a car ride. I already sucked up my pride when I told Ben he was free to get Clara's phone number the night of my family's layover. Wasn't that enough? I don't think I can handle having to tell him how to win her over.

"You know I'm not used to women like her. I'll fuck it up for sure without your help."

I blow out a breath, my hand on the handle of the door. I'll do it for Clara, because she does not deserve to come down here and spend all her time at sports bars where Ben spends more time with fans than he does with her. If she likes him, which she must if she's still talking to him, then

I'll give him my two cents on what I'd do if Clara was a girl I wanted to impress.

"Listen. Clara isn't into the scholarly types. Hello, I'm her fucking best friend. I went to school on a football scholarship, not for my grades."

"But still, man, you're smarter than me."

"First of all, she won't like it if you keep putting yourself down. She agreed for you to have her phone number. That must mean she's into you. And she's cool as hell with sports and bars. She can eat more wings than me most nights, but if I was going to date her, I'd take her to a nice restaurant outside of town, or get a private room. Give her the opportunity to dress up and get to know you. Maybe take a walk around the pier after."

Clara and I have done all the tourist stuff ten times since I've been here.

"Show her why you love San Francisco," I add.

He nods a bunch of times. "Yeah, okay."

"And I'd hold off on Kozy Kar until the third date or something."

Kozy Kar is a theme bar that Ben loves, but it's got a weird vibe that includes throwbacks from the seventies up to the nineties. You can drink on a waterbed, and there are stripper poles and posters of naked women everywhere. What do I know though? Maybe Clara would like it.

"Really? I always take women there. I think it's cool and there are all the dark corners to make out."

I swallow hard at the thought of him making out with her.

"Well, she's not your average girl." I open the car door, say goodbye to the driver, and head into the arena, saying hello to security.

Ben's quick to catch up to me. "Are you sure you're okay with this?"

I stop before entering the locker room. "Just... I mean, she's someone really important to me." That truth remains, regardless of how long it's been since we really talked.

He puts his big bear paw of a hand on my shoulder. "I know, X. I'm not in this to get in her panties. I'm getting older now and I'm looking to settle down."

I raise both eyebrows.

He chuckles. "I'm not *just* looking for fun anymore, that's what I mean."

I nod and open the locker room door. "Her favorite food is dessert. Get her anything to satisfy her sweet tooth after the meal and it will be a success."

His smile grows while my stomach grows nauseated. "Thanks, X."

He heads to his locker, and I do the same. My mood grows sourer when I see the guy sitting next to my space.

Lee fucking Burrows. The new quarterback brought onto the team to take my place should I not be able to perform this year.

"Hey, Xavier," he says with a smile. The guy is so laid back it drives me crazy. The worst part is, he's smart as shit, probably already knows the playbook.

He got traded at the end of the season, and I can't deny from the tapes I've watched, he should do well. He showed that he could probably take my place in a heartbeat.

Which gives me two goals this season. Further secure my position on this team. Show them why they signed me to a huge five-year deal two years ago. And second, win back my best friend.

Chapter Two

"But I'm proud of you."

Clara

I walk into my sister's bookstore, The Story Shop, trying to ignore the chalkboard sign outside the neighboring brewery, Truth or Dare. Today is the first Sunday game day for football, and the San Francisco Kingsmen are playing. Two years ago, I would've had Xavier's number nine written on my cheeks and been decked out in his red-and-gold jersey.

Now, I'm going to help Presley do inventory for her store.

The shop is quiet when I enter, and I take a moment to admire her display of fall books with pumpkins and leaves scattered around.

I didn't grow up with Presley. She didn't come into my life until after both my parents had passed away. This used to be my mom's sewing store and was left to both of us when she died. That's when Presley arrived in town and surprised everyone, including me. Lots of people think we're twins, except for our hair colors. We recently flipped them around though. She's allowed hers to go back to our original brown while I've dyed mine blonde.

"Pres!" I call and venture toward the back of the store.

Ohhh.

God, yes.

Harder.

I close my eyes and my head falls back. It's nice that my married sister, who recently had a baby, is getting some, but I can't say I'm overjoyed to hear a play-by-play. Or I'm just a bit envious.

CAAADDEEEE...

I quickly walk toward the door, but it springs open before I can leave. The bell goes off louder than when I entered because Jed Greene is a moose-in-a-library kind of guy.

He stops in his tracks when he sees me and runs his hand through his hair. "Oh... hey, Clara."

The familiar awkwardness consumes the space we're sharing because Jed has no idea what happened between Xavier and me and therefore seems to have no idea how to act when I'm around. He constantly treats me as if my dog just died.

"They're busy."

His gaze sears a path to the back room. "I figured. We're working our asses off, and Molly needs to go home. She's still constantly throwing up. She was only helping today because it's crazy—" He abruptly stops talking and diverts his attention away from me.

"Because it's the first game of the season?" I prompt so he knows he can discuss Xavier in front of me.

He shoves his hands in his pockets and nods.

"Busy is good." I thumb toward the back. "I think they're done anyway."

Just then, Cade and Presley come out of the back room with their baby, Leighton, fast asleep in a car seat.

"Seriously? You do it with the baby in the room?" Jed shakes his head and scowls.

Cade and Presley look at one another, my sister's cheeks reddening as she realizes we heard them.

"Next time we'll ask you to babysit," Cade says. "She's sleeping, dipshit."

Jed rolls his eyes. "Still not right."

"Talk to me after Molly delivers." Cade kisses his wife's lips. "Have fun." Then he dips down and kisses Leighton on the forehead and whispers something. "Clara." Cade winks at me as he passes by, and I can't help but see his resemblance to Xavier.

As if my life couldn't be more screwed up, my sister's husband is Xavier's oldest brother and Jed is Xavier's stepbrother. Although in the Greene family, no one thinks of anyone else as a step anything.

"Bye, Clara," Jed says.

As they leave, Jed rambles on about scarring Leighton for life and how her first word will be harder.

"Can you lock the door?" Presley asks and places Leighton's car seat carrier on the table in the children's area.

I lock the door and remove my light jacket and purse, placing them by the cash register. "Where do you want me to start?"

As the words leave my mouth, Jed's voice sounds through the shared wall of the brewery and the bookstore. It sounds as if he's on a microphone or a loudspeaker or something.

"I think they're going extra hard this year because of Hank." Presley gives me her sorrowful half smile. Otherwise known as a pitiful expression.

Hank Greene has prostate cancer and is currently undergoing treatment. Although the prognosis is good, cancer is a scary thing. I should know—it's what took our mother. I watched her fade away for months, her once-vibrant body turning frail, all while she kept her biggest secret from me.

Sometimes I'm still not sure I've forgiven her for never telling me I had an older sister that she and my dad had given up for adoption. But how does one make peace with a dead person?

"What are they doing?" I walk over to join Presley in the children's area.

"Raffles. If you guess the right score at the end of each quarter, you get free food or drinks." She shrugs as if it's nothing big, but the fact that there's a microphone and the place is packed says that's not the case.

I remember Hank's face when Xavier was drafted. Xavier invited Hank, Marla, and me to the draft, and when Xavier's name was called first and he walked up to that podium, Hank put his arm around my shoulders and whispered, "Can you believe it? Our boy is going to be a household name."

Chills rack my body as the words "our boy" repeat in my head. Well, he's not our boy. He's just Hank's boy now.

"Let's start with the kids' section." Presley has her laptop and a stack of inventory papers in hand, and I distract myself from my memories and join her.

I sit on the floor. I'm always Presley's helper for inventory. Once, Cade tried to take my place, but they didn't get much done. I'm positive that's when Leighton was conceived.

Before we can begin, she starts up with me. "So?" She doesn't look up from her computer.

"What?" I feign ignorance even though I know what she's inquiring about.

"Did you return Xavier's text?"

I sigh and shake my head. "No. What do I say and what the hell does it even mean? Just 'you looked good'... like the demise of our friendship is of little consequence. Or is it 'you looked good' and maybe I shouldn't have done what I did? Or is it my friend wanted your number so maybe you're worth a try?" Even I hear the hurt and anger that still lives in my tone whenever we talk about this.

"Maybe he really realizes how crappy what he did was. Cade said Hank told him he talked to Xavier that night."

I put up my hand. "I don't want to know."

"From what I understand, he misses you." She bites the inside of her lip. "And I know you miss him."

"Pres, what happened to us is what happens to every girl and boy best friend where one person's feelings change. There's no going back to how it was."

Presley is the only Greene who knows anything that went on, but the story isn't unique—two childhood best friends allowed the lines to blur one night, only for one friend to regret what happened. Let's just say *I* wasn't the one who regretted our night together. Add on what he did the next night, and it's going to be hard to come back from that.

"You guys had such a close friendship. He helped you through Mom and Dad's deaths. I don't care what he says, he has deep feelings for you." She punches away on the keyboard.

"Yeah, *friendship* feelings. I saw him through his own mother's death, so of course he saw me through both my parents passing. I'm not denying that he loves me, it's just a different love. Not the kind of love that was just happening with you and Cade in the back room."

A sigh falls from her lips. This is Presley, the optimistic girl who found love and sees everything with rose-colored glasses now.

I've witnessed Xavier's way with women over the years. I could've predicted his and Giulia's breakup. He'll never be all in with someone. He won't let himself grow that close to someone else.

"That wasn't love. That was I'm horny and that rarely happens now that my nipples are raw from breastfeeding and I'm still carrying twenty extra pounds. I should've known when I put on the overalls. They get him every time." The smile that slowly lights up her face is one of pure love.

My heart pricks. I do want that. "Well, it's not something I have."

"Which is why you're going to continue talking to that Ben guy."

Seems Presley's on to round two. When she can't get me to agree on Xavier, she moves on to Ben, Xavier's teammate who's been texting me nonstop. So much so that I feel like I'm running out of things to say to him. "He's hot."

He's big. A wide reciever who, yeah, has the usual arrogance of a professional football player. That adds to his sex appeal, but he has a reputation. Maybe I'm just a conquest, get the librarian in bed. Or worse, what if he's playing mind games with Xavier? I don't think he'd do that, but I don't know Ben or their friendship well enough to really know.

"Did you make plans to see one another?" Presley's typing in the numbers from the sheet I just handed her, and I fill in the next one as I account for each of the books.

"He wants me to go down for the Seahawks game."

"Fun. I bet he'll give you great seats."

"I wish you could come."

We both look at Leighton, and Presley frowns. "Sorry. What about Mandi or Chevelle?"

I look up from the sheet. "Because it's harder to be around them. They're his sister and stepsister."

"But if you take them, they can hang with Xavier while you go on a date with Ben."

She has a point, but I shrug. "It's weird."

A roar from the brewery echoes into the quiet shop and Leighton squirms for a second before Presley rocks the car seat to soothe her. "I think they scored."

I nod and write down how many *When the Sidewalk Ends* books she has—trying not to think about whether it was a pass or handoff by Xavier and wonder how many yards and whether the announcers are singing his praises.

"I'm happy for him. I really am. Xavier's got everything he ever wanted in life. The fame, the recognition, the money. It's every dream he's ever told me he had. I guess I was naive to think that he'd look at me in a different way after... that he wouldn't see the Clara Harrison in pigtails who built forts with him in the woods and competed over who could ride their bike to the square faster."

Presley abandons her computer and puts her arm around my shoulders. "He's stupid for not knowing that you're the best woman he could ever hope to find." She rocks me back and forth.

"Pres?"

"Yeah?"

"I'm nauseous."

She laughs and stops rocking us. "Force of habit, sorry." I lay my head on her shoulder. "It's time to move on though. It's been two years, and if anything, he spit in your face with that whole show when he paraded Giulia around Sunrise Bay. If you have even a small bit of interest in Ben, I say you go for it. Give the guy a chance."

With a nod, I pull out my phone before I can change my mind. My thumbs hover over the screen. He won't get the message until after the game. The crowd groans next door, so I assume that something didn't go the Kingsmen's way.

I read his text one more time.

Ben: I'll pay for your flight. Let me show you the San Francisco I love.

Presley is reading the screen over my shoulder. "That's cute."

"I know San Francisco like Sunrise Bay because Xavier and I have done everything there over the years."

She knocks her shoulder with mine. "Clara, open mind. Give the poor guy a chance."

With a sigh, I stare at the blinking cursor and finally type out my message.

I'd love to. Let me check my schedule at work and get back to you.

There's some relief that he can't answer me right away.

Presley raises her eyebrows.

"What?"

"Nice way to give yourself a possible out with work. But I'm proud of you."

Leighton stirs, so Presley rises off the floor and unstraps her from the carrier. Leighton slowly peers at me with the same eyes a lot of the Greene family has. Yeah, I can't deny that I want a family.

Presley's right—I need to move on. I'm just not sure Ben is the one I need to move on with. I guess that's why I need to get to know him.

Chapter Three

Xavier

A month later and the Seahawks game is here. More importantly, Clara is coming tonight to spend the weekend with Ben. In fact, he's at the airport, picking her up right now.

"I have a package for you," Kerbie says, stopping me from just waving and walking into the elevator.

I detour back to his desk and he scours through the packages to find it.

"No Mr. Noughton today?" Kerbie asks while inspecting the packages.

"No. Just me."

He lifts the package as I'm about to say I'll come back down for it. I'm fairly sure it's the jacket I ordered online last week. "Here it is!"

The package is smaller than I'd expect a jacket to come in.

"Thanks, Kerbie."

I head to the elevator, press the up button, and wait for it to arrive. I inspect the return address to see Greywall, Alaska. A PO box, nonetheless. Greywall borders my small hometown of Sunrise Bay, but I don't know anyone there who would have my address to send me a package.

The mystery of the contents weighs on me the entire

16

elevator ride up to my condo, so the minute I'm inside, I drop my bag and tear it open.

Inside the package are cookies from my favorite bakery in Lake Starlight. Each one has frosting that reads *Beat the Hawks*. Who would have sent this to me? Only one person from back home would go to this much trouble and she's the one coming tonight to spend time with another man. Could this be a peace offering? Even though she's yet to respond to my text message?

I sit on the couch, eating one of the cookies, and my mind can't help but remember how things went bad with us. I'm not sure how we'll ever get back to where we were.

I woke up with a start, after having the best night's sleep of my life, to find a naked Clara next to me. Things had gotten out of hand the night before, and with the dawn came a rush of regrets I couldn't shake.

I saw the look in her eyes and the soft smile that conveyed all her emotions. She was hopeful this was a turning point for us. Of course Clara would lay her cards down for me. She was never one to hide how she felt, especially with me. And what did I do? I hurried out of the bed, mumbling something about coffee.

Before she had time to get her naked body out of my bed and put on some clothes, I was out the door. Once I reached the eleva-tor, I bent over and breathed for the first time since I'd woken. Or at least it felt that way.

What the hell had I done? Did I ruin decades of friendship because I couldn't control myself?

I'd lost all control when I placed my lips on hers. It was as though someone had unleashed me from the restraints that had always kept me from crossing that line with her.

But there was no way we could do it again. She'd have expec-tations. Expectations I sure as shit couldn't fulfill. Clara deserved someone who wouldn't run out on her first thing in the morning.

She deserved someone who enjoyed hiking the trails after the snow melted and wanted to go into town and have twenty mini-conversations with the townspeople. Someone who could be beside her while she did it. Clara Harrison is Sunrise Bay, a fixture in our small town, and I was the one who got out.

We needed to go straight back to being best friends and pretend like this had never happened, otherwise I could lose her. And I couldn't lose Clara from my life.

I headed down to the coffee shop on the corner where the barista knew me. She instantly smiled and typed in my order, and she frowned when I gave her Clara's order of a chai latte with oat milk. I'd always suspected the barista had a crush on me, and I guessed I'd confirmed for her that a woman had spent the night at my place. Not that that was a new thing for me. Clara wasn't the first woman who'd been in my bed, but she was the first I'd bought coffee for the morning after.

By the time I'd stopped to get Clara's favorite donut and open my condo door, she was sitting in the family room, dressed in my T-shirt and probably nothing on underneath. The door shut and we stared at one another from opposite sides of the room for the briefest moment before I flicked my gaze away. I felt sick. I'd really fucked up.

"I got you your favorite donut. The Cocoa Pebbles one." I busied myself in the kitchen, grabbing plates and setting them up.

"X?" The hairs on the back of my neck stood on edge with how close her voice was to me. "Talk to me. Please."

All the tension in my shoulders dropped and I slowly turned her way with two plates in my hands.

"It's okay to be scared. I am too." She rounded the long island that floated in the middle of my kitchen, and she was coming right to me.

My throat closed up and I had no idea how I would say it to her, but I had to. Sure, she would be hurt, but she'd get over it and we'd go on with how things had been. If I tried to be with her romantically, knowing there was no way to make it work, then I'd end up breaking her heart and we'd never recover from that.

"But running out on me—"

"We can't do this, Clara." I spat out the words without any regard, and I swear she flinched. "I mean. I love you. You're my best friend. I'm not sure what happened last night, but that can never happen again. It was a mistake."

She blinked. Then she stepped back. I wanted to grab her as if I were a life preserver and could save her from the huge swells caused by me. "But you said... you said it was everything..." She turned on her heels and rushed away, calling out over her shoulder, "I'm going to get dressed."

Like the idiot I was, I waited five whole minutes to go after her and found her packing her suitcase. My T-shirt was long gone, and she was in jogger pants and a sweatshirt. "You don't have to leave."

She didn't even grant me a glance. "This is awkward. I mean, I thought we were..."

"Come here." I patted the spot next to me on the bed and she sat down. "You know how I feel about serious relationships. I should've stopped us, but I guess things got carried away."

To my surprise, she agreed. "They did, but..." She turned to face me, one leg bent and resting on the bed and her other leg stretched to the floor. "I liked it. I mean, I enjoyed myself last night."

I chuckled. "And you think I didn't? Of course I did, but it's not like we're meant to be friends with benefits. Eventually lines would blur, and you would get hurt." I took her hand. "You know I can't lose you."

Clara was my one constant, besides my family. She was the one who cheered for me and didn't let my insecurities creep in, making me abandon my dreams. She was the one who told me *when I was being an arrogant prick and kept me grounded. She was the one who let me relish in the fact that my hard work had gotten me to where I was and said I should be proud. So there's no chance in hell I'm losing her because my dick took over my thinking for me one night.*

When she still hadn't said anything after a full minute, I asked, "What is it, Clara?"

"It's just... I felt something... something more than friendship last night."

I sighed and pushed my hand through my hair. "We can only ever be friends."

"I wished you'd realized that last night when I tried to stop us." There was anger lacing her tone and I understood it. Hell, I deserved it.

"I was caught up in the moment. I'm sorry. But I can't lose you."

"You'll never lose me, Xavier." She wrapped her arms around me. "Never. We're best friends. Always."

Her voice shook when she said best friends and I knew Clara way too well to not know that I'd hurt her. That she'd thought because it was her, it meant something different. That there was a possibility I'd wake up a different guy. Not the one cynical about falling in love, but one who believed in happily ever afters and that life was full of rainbows and sunshine.

"So, you'll stay?" I asked selfishly. "We have that party tonight."

"As long as that coffee in there is my chai latte."

Her smile righted my world again, and it was as if the two of us hadn't had one of the sexiest nights in my existence. Despite what I was saying, I knew I'd be reliving that night for the rest of my life.

For the whole day, I saw Clara in a different light. When she pulled her hair into a ponytail, I remembered my lips traveling the length of her neck. Or when she crossed her legs, I remembered those legs curled around my waist, the heat of her core pressed to my hardness. And when she came out of my guest bedroom wearing a dress that was way too short, I almost lost that ounce of self-control I'd always kept intact when it came to Clara—until last night.

We headed to the engagement party for my teammate who'd already been married twice and thought the third time was the charm. I had my doubts, but I tended to not be the one to ask. The bar was packed, but they had a back room reserved just for our party.

I opened the curtained-off area and Clara walked in first. My eyes fell to her ass until Ben distracted me by yelling my name from across the room. Before I had time to say hello to anyone else, he had Clara in a big bear hug, her feet dangling off the floor. I wanted to growl like a protective papa bear, but I reminded myself that Clara wasn't mine.

The party was in full swing, and although Clara had said all the right things to assure me our friendship was fine, there was an awkwardness between us that had never been present before.

We played pool, darts, and drank casually. One thing I loved about Clara was her willingness to venture off and not be stuck at my hip. Then again, she'd known some of these guys as long as I have.

A tall blonde sauntered up to my table and signaled to the empty seat. "May I?"

"Have at it." I slid the stool out for her and caught a glimpse of her micro minidress. There was more fabric on my board shorts.

"Xavier, right?"

I nodded and sipped my beer. "Yeah."

"My friends bet me I wouldn't have the guts to come over here." She put her hand out between us. "I'm Juliette."

I took her limp hand. "Nice to meet you, Juliette. Can I get you a drink?"

She twirled her hair with her finger, and I sighed because Clara and I always made fun of girls who messed with their hair as a way to try to attract a man. But these are the girls who know the score. They know there's no forever when you pick up a professional football player in a bar.

I lifted my arm to draw the attention of the waitress, but while I scanned the area, my eyes stopped on Clara. Actually, they stopped on Ben standing way too close to Clara. Flashes of last night came to mind.

"Excuse me," I said to Juliette.

"But the drink..."

"Sorry," I barked at her, setting my focus on my best friend and teammate.

They were talking with Ashton, and he was going on and on about some girl who wouldn't leave his apartment.

"Hey, guys," I said, interrupting. "Clara, can I talk to you?"

Ashton continued on with the story.

She put up her finger. "Just a minute."

"Actually, X, I gotta talk to you." Ben nodded away from the group.

I was going to talk to Clara about staying away from Ben, but I guess it'll be Ben I'll talk to.

When we were in the bathroom hallway, I asked, "What's up?"

"I just wanted to make sure it was cool with you if I ask Clara out. I know you guys are, like, best friends and stuff."

I hadn't expected this. I didn't think Ben would do the honorable thing like asking me if it was okay. Images of Clara naked and writhing under me the night before flashed through my mind. Her smooth legs sliding up my waist. Her soft palms running down my back. Her begging and pleading for me to never stop.

"Yeah…"

He slapped me on the back. "Thanks, man."

"NO!" *I swallowed past the lump in my throat.* "I mean, I'm not cool with it. She's not going to be one of your girls to tell a story about like Ashton."

I walked out of the hallway. Ben's mouth was open, but he didn't fight me on it. I knew he wouldn't.

I headed in Clara's direction to get her out of here, but Juliette stepped in front of me.

"Hey, you," *she said, her finger running down my chest.* "You bought me a Sex On The Beach."

"Great. Enjoy." *I stepped around her and overheard her mumbling her displeasure, but I couldn't care less.*

My bigger problem was that Ben was now giving all his attention to a brunette and Clara was glaring daggers at me.

"I'm beat. Let's go." *I placed my hand on her elbow, but she pried it away from me.*

"What did you tell Ben?"

"Nothing."

She turned to me, her shoulders square. A pissed-off Clara was never good. "That's funny, Xavier, because he came over to me just now and said he was sorry, he really liked me, but bro code and all that."

"Please, you'd be his flavor of the night. I saved you." *I nodded toward the door.* "Let's go."

"No. I'm not going. And maybe I want to be his flavor of the night. Did you ever think of that? It's actually none of your business."

"You are always my business."

She slammed her drink on the table and leaned in closer. I was sure some of my teammates were watching. "Let me get this straight. You've decided you don't want me, but no one else can have me either, is that it?"

"No, that's not it." I shook my head, not understanding what she was getting at.

"That's exactly it! We're friends, so sure, you can have an opinion on who I choose to date or hook up with, but you do not get to dictate my decisions for me. Nor do you get to be so heavy handed that you go behind my back and try to prevent me from even getting to make the decision in the first place. Especially after you tossed me aside."

"I thought we were on the same page that last night was a mistake. That this is what's best?"

"Yes, you conveniently decided that after we slept together. Bravo." She shook her head and I saw tears pooling in her eyes. "You don't know anything, Xavier Greene. Just go back to your girl. I'm so done with you."

She stomped away and I left not soon after, taking a long enough walk around San Francisco that when I got back to my condo, she was already gone. Needless to say, there wasn't a note waiting for me.

Chapter Four

Clara

I'm used to a certain kind of treatment when I come into town to visit Xavier. Usually, I was greeted by a driver, but if Xavier was available, he'd always wait for me right after security.

So after finally accepting Ben's invitation to visit him this weekend, I'm surprised to find neither as I descend the escalator into arrivals. No Ben and no driver holding my handwritten name on a sign. He said he'd handle everything, including meeting me at the airport.

Maybe Ben's at baggage claim? I check the overhead screen and find my designated baggage carousel. I still see no one. As I wait for the luggage to arrive, I pull out my phone, but there's no text message from Ben.

Finally, the conveyor belt starts moving and all the passengers from my flight descend as though we're at the doors of Walmart on Black Friday at opening time. I'm in luck because my bag is the fourth one out, so I grab it and quickly wheel it out of the way before I'm trampled by someone.

As soon as I step outside, the sun hits my face and I relish the warmer air for a moment, forgetting how awkward it is that I've come down here to spend the weekend with Xavier's teammate.

A loud honking makes me stop soaking in vitamin *D* to see what is going on. A huge truck pulls up in front of me and stops abruptly. I squint, although the dark shadow the truck has created by blocking out the sun helps me see that the monstrosity in front of me is being driven by Ben.

The traffic officer is power walking toward us with a whistle in his mouth, blowing it over and over again. "Sir! Sir!"

Ben doesn't bother looking at him, instead climbing down from his enormous truck and rounding the front with a huge smile. "I worried I missed you."

He reaches for my bag, and we do an awkward dance of do we or don't we hug hello. I end up almost patting him on the back as though I'm hugging a stranger. Meanwhile, I feel eyes on me, the bystanders who just realized who the man driving the truck is. Maybe this is why Xavier always had a car waiting and ready to whisk us away.

"*Sir!*" The traffic officer bends at the waist to catch his breath. "You cannot... park... here."

Ben tosses my bag in the back as though he's hurling a shot put down a field. "Sorry. I just had to pick up my friend." Ben winks at me and disappointment spreads through my chest that nothing lights up inside me. Then he puts his hand out toward the traffic officer. "Ben Noughton."

The traffic officer's eyes widen, and he steps back in surprise. "Oh, I'm sorry, I didn't recognize..."

Ben puts his hand on the stout man's shoulder. "It's okay. No harm done. Mind if I get going?"

"Sure, sure." The traffic officer looks enraptured just to be standing in Ben's presence.

It shouldn't surprise me. Having spent so much time with Xavier, I've seen all the reactions—crying hysterically, pure joy, and everything in between.

"Great." Ben walks to the passenger door and opens it for me.

A few passengers coming out of the airport approach and ask him for an autograph. I smile to let him know it's fine, I'll wait. Another thing I'm used to.

But Ben shakes his head. "Nah, we've got to get going. Sorry."

I step onto the runner of his truck and pull myself up by the *oh-shit* handle at the top of the door. No need for him to help me.

"Now you spoiled my fun. I planned on having to put my hand on your ass." He laughs and shuts the door, then comes around to his side and climbs in.

I feel as though I'm in a semitruck with how high up we are. "Is this yours?"

He nods. "I usually keep it in the parking garage because driving it around San Fran is a pain in the ass, but I figured I'd take Shelby out for the special occasion." He lovingly taps the dashboard.

"Special occasion?"

He starts the truck back up and the noise floods the cab. "Yeah, you finally agreed to come visit." He winks again, and once more, my stomach doesn't react. Putting the truck in gear, he presses on the gas and pulls out of the airport arrival area.

"Thank you for coming to get me." I start the conversation after a few moments of him singing along with the country music on the radio.

"I never would've left you to fend for yourself." He smiles at me.

I smile back and we ride in silence for a beat as my thoughts wander. I have to assume this monstrous truck and the fact that he's listening to country music means he's from somewhere in the south, or maybe Montana or Wyoming. I know I shouldn't stereotype—everyone thinks Alaskans live in igloos.

I shift in my seat a little to face him better. "I've never asked you. Where are you from?"

"Nebraska," he says. "Midwest boy."

"Did you buy this truck when you got to San Francisco or drive it here?"

"Drove it. I didn't realize I'd have no use for it. I rarely take Shelby anywhere unless I decide to disappear from the city for a day."

That fact catches my attention. "Do you do that often?"

He shrugs. "Not as much as I'd like to. During the season, it's pretty hard, and lately, I've been traveling in the off-season. Gotta spend this money somehow, you know?"

I chuckle. "I'm a librarian in a small town, so I can't really relate."

He stops at a light and the pedestrians crossing gawk at the truck as if it's a UFO. One kid stops right in front of the grill with wide eyes and an open mouth.

"That's right. The librarian thing. Tell me, what's that like?"

"Um..." My job isn't all that interesting. I mean, I find it fulfilling to help people find the information they're seeking, or when I pick out a book for a young reader and they first discover the joy of reading. But I don't think someone like Ben would find anything about my job exciting. "It's pretty much what you'd expect. A lot of researching, helping people. Mostly the elderly people in our community and the very young ones. Seems most in the middle have discovered e-books. Lately, I've been trying to figure out ways to draw them in. I actually started—"

"Here we are. I figure we'll get your bags, if you want to

change your clothes or whatever, then we'll head out, find something to do in the city? I have practice tomorrow, but then I have plans for us to have dinner."

Was he even listening when he interrupted me?

The doorman opens my door before I can dwell further on that thought and his eyes open in shock. "Miss Harrison?" He looks around. "Where is Mr. Greene?"

"Hello, Kerbie." I accept his hand and step down from the truck.

"She's with me, Kerb," Ben says and grabs my bag in the back. "We'll be back in no time if anyone comes by causing trouble."

"Mr. Noughton, you cannot leave this truck here. We've been over the rules. If the police come by, I cannot stop them from ticketing you."

"Tell them it's Ben Noughton's truck and if they don't ticket me, I'll get them tickets to the next game."

Kerbie blows out a breath and opens the door of the building. "Sure thing, Mr. Noughton. Miss Harrison." He nods and gestures for me to walk inside.

"Thanks, Kerbie." Once we're in the lobby, a suffocating feeling envelops me. "Ben, I assumed I'd stay at a hotel."

His shoulders slouch and he stares at the floor for a moment. "Shit. I messed up, didn't I?" He looks up, his blue eyes full of genuine concern. "I wasn't assuming anything. I promise. I'll sleep on the couch, and you can have the bedroom. I only bought a one-bedroom since I don't have a lot of family who would come and visit me, and I didn't grow up just throwing money out the window. But damn it, I should've booked a hotel."

"It's—"

"Kerbie," Ben says and walks away from me without

letting me finish. "Could you call a few hotels and see if there're any rooms available for Clara?"

Kerbie's dark eyebrows shoot up, but then he looks at me and nods. "Sure thing, but may I remind you there's a lot going on in the city this weekend? Not the least of which is your game tomorrow. My guess is it'll be hard to find a room at a decent hotel."

Ben's mouth turns into a straight line, and he shakes his head. "I'm such a dumbass."

"No, it's fine. Honestly." I wave off his concern.

Kerbie rushes from his desk area to the doors, and even before Kerbie greets him, I feel his presence. "Mr. Greene, welcome back."

"Thanks, Kerbie." I hear his shoes skid to a stop on the marble floor. "Oh yeah," he says as if he forgot I was coming this weekend.

"Yes, Miss Harrison is here." Kerbie uses his chipper voice. The fake one usually reserved for Mrs. Ascot on the twelfth floor and her two Pomeranians.

"I see that. How are you, Clara?" Xavier's so stiff and formal with me. I hate it.

"Good. Just got in."

He glances at my suitcase sitting at Ben's feet and looks away. "Just had to bring Shelby out, huh?"

"You know it. Figured I'd introduce the two women in my life to each other." Ben laughs and Xavier coughs, then clears his throat.

Thank God the elevator arrives then. They each signal for me to enter first. They follow me in, and Xavier presses the buttons for both Ben's floor and his own. Before the doors shut, Kerbie waves goodbye.

And then it's just the three of us.

When no one says a word, Xavier asks, "How are things

in Sunrise Bay?"

Ben seems occupied on his phone, and I want to tug on his arm to get him to show some sort of interest.

"Good. Leighton is getting bigger. She has your eyes."

Xavier holds my gaze for a moment.

"I mean Cade's eyes. The Greenes' eyes."

He nods. "Yeah."

"Chevelle and Cam got into an argument at the marina the other day. She ended up pushing him over the edge of the pier and into the water."

Xavier snickers. "You don't think..."

I nod. "I do. What do you think Fisher is gonna do?"

He chuckles again. The deep-in-his-throat one. The honest one that only talking about his family can pull out. "He's gonna go ballistic. What about that funding you were pitching for the library? Tell me Gavin came through?"

The town mayor, Gavin Price, is married to Xavier's step-sister, Posey. I went to him with plans for an extension on the library so we could have a dedicated technology section. Right now there's one computer that's available for patrons to use and people are often waiting for someone to finish. I envision having many more, along with tablets and other technology as it becomes available and even hosting tech classes for seniors and young children who don't have access to the technology at home or at school.

"I have a meeting with him next week. I'll have to do fundraising."

"I'll give you the money and you can name it after me." Ben elbows me and laughs. I guess he is paying attention.

"No, I want everyone in the town to help out. It's to benefit all of us." I turn him down, though I'm sure Ben was only kidding.

The elevator stops on Ben's floor, and the tension grows

so thick I can barely breathe. It feels as if the air I'm pulling in is as thick as potato soup.

"You're staying here?" Xavier asks.

"Yeah," Ben answers for me.

Xavier's eyes find mine. "Oh."

"He forgot to book a room and it's probably too late to find one, so..." I don't know why I'm giving him way more information than he deserves.

"You can stay in your room at my place. I mean..." He runs his hand down the back of his head, pulling at his neck. "If you'd prefer."

Ben glances at me and I look up at him as he says, "It's up to you."

I came all this way to spend the weekend with Ben, but I don't really know him. I trust that he's a good guy because he's Xavier's teammate and friend. Has been for years. But spending the weekend with him already has me feeling a little nervous and uncomfortable and that was before I knew I'd be staying with him. Then again, I'm not really talking to Xavier either.

"We're good," I say.

Xavier releases his hold on the door open button. "Have a great time then."

The doors close and all I want to do is rush back to him, but instead I smile at Ben. "Show me your place."

Chapter Five

Xavier

The minute I step into my condo, I toss my bag on the couch and go to stand at the window that overlooks the bay and the bridge. Ben doesn't have this view. Nor does he have my contract to get this view.

I run my hand through my hair. "Fuck," I murmur, pissed that I'm comparing the two of us.

I'm the one who told Clara I didn't want to be with her that way after we slept together. *I'm* the one who's let two years go by without my best friend by my side. *I'm* the one who said I was cool with the two of them dating.

Walking into the kitchen, I grab a glass and a bottle of scotch and pour myself a hefty amount. It's Friday after all. I have a light practice tomorrow before our game Sunday. I've been nervous all week, which is weird because it's not like I'm a rookie. It must be because Lee Burrows is breathing down my neck, gunning for my position.

While I sip my scotch, my phone dings in my pocket. I pull it out of my track pants and see Sessilee's name flash across the screen. I hit *Ignore*, hoping she gets the hint. Even though Giulia has moved on from me to some Italian race car driver, that doesn't mean she wouldn't spit fire if I dated her friend. And that's if I was even interested.

A ping comes next, which means she didn't get the

message, but I'm surprised when Ben's name appears on my screen.

> I don't think Clara is comfortable here. I really fucked up with the hotel thing. Not sure what I was thinking.

I refrain from telling him he was thinking that Clara's like all the other girls he's used to having fly in for the weekend. The ones who want to sleep with him. I have no idea if Clara does or doesn't, but the idea alone grates on me like sandpaper. Still, she's not usually one to sleep with someone she barely knows.

> Just go ask her. I'm sure she's fine if she says she is.

A small protective part of me wonders if what I said is the truth. Clara never wants to hurt anyone's feelings and sometimes that puts her in awkward situations. Ones I would usually save her from.

> Where should I take her tonight?

It's no secret that Ben isn't very suave with the ladies. Sure, he gets laid plenty—he's a professional football player. But the guy was born and raised in a small Nebraska town and raised by his dad and his two brothers. He's just a little rough around the edges, and I'm not sure he knows how to wine and dine a woman. Truth is, he's probably never had to.

> Take her to the new restaurant in Jackson Square.

> I'll never get in. Not to mention, the cost.

I chuckle and sip my scotch. Sure, Ben doesn't make what I do, but he's not a paycheck away from living in a cardboard box on the street. The man has done more than well for himself.

> I'll get you in.

Ben obviously didn't take my advice about showing Clara what he loves most about the city.

> You're a lifesaver.

I nod, finishing my scotch.

> I'll call now. It might be a late reservation depending.

> Hey, do you want to come? I'm sure we can find you a date to double date or even just us three would be fun.

I read his text a few more times. Is he really asking me to join him on his date? Would I even want to? The idea of watching the two of them together makes me want to bleach my eyeballs, but so does the idea of sitting around here and imagining what might be going on.

> Come on. It's kind of awkward right now. I have nothing to talk to her about. She's so smart.

Ben has already confessed to me his insecurity when it comes to Clara. She isn't his normal type of girl, but Ben can hold his own with her.

> Ask Ashton and Kara. Clara and Kara got along well that one night.

(GIF with an arrow hitting a bull's-eye).
You're a genius. Calling him now.

> So that's a reservation for four.

Thanks X

I search for the number of the restaurant and dial it up.

A woman answers on the first ring. "Hello, thank you for calling Hillstone. This is Natalia. How can I help you?"

"Hi, Natalia, this is Xavier Greene, quarterback for the—"

She giggles. "I am well aware of who you are."

"Great. I wondered if you had any tables for four open tonight. I understand it's short notice but—"

"Let me check. We are booked two months ahead at this point, but being who you are... well... just give me a moment."

"Sure. Thank you."

She puts me on hold, and I pour myself another scotch. Not sure I'll be able to handle being three floors above Clara and Ben. My mind is going crazy, wondering what the hell they're doing down there.

Natalia comes back on the line. "The chef would love to host you and your guests. He's going to put you at the chef's table in the kitchen."

"Oh... great." I hadn't planned on being there, but since we're being seated at the chef's table, I suppose I'll have to be. "Please thank the chef for me and we'll see you around seven?"

"Perfect. We look forward to seeing you, Mr. Greene."

I hang up, and instead of going back and forth with Ben on text message, I call him.

"Hey," he answers in a whisper.

My eyebrows furrow. "Is something wrong?"

"No, no. Just don't want her to know I had to use you to get us a table. Hold on, I'm going into the bathroom. Be right back, Clara." I hear a door shut. "Okay. Did you get a table? Ashton can't come. I'm thinking about asking Damon."

"No need. The restaurant thinks I'm going to be there, so I have to scrounge up a date. But it's the chef's table at seven."

He goes back to whispering. "Chef's table! Man, you're the best."

"I'll see you there, okay?"

"You're a lifesaver. Thank you so much."

"No problem."

We hang up and I scroll through the list of contacts on my phone. It's three in the afternoon, how the hell am I gonna find a date?

I DO FIND A DATE, but Sessilee's not my first choice by a long shot. I press the elevator button to head down to my car to pick her up at her hotel before meeting Clara and Ben at Hillstone.

Jesus. Just thinking about their names together as though they're a real couple makes me nauseated. Even if I only have myself to blame.

On one hand, I'm pissed I ever agreed to this shit. Second, if Ben wants to date Clara, he should plan the night his damn self. I shouldn't be stuck playing wingman to him when I should be going over game film and the playbook in preparation for Sunday's game.

The elevator door opens, and I hit the ground floor button, but surprise surprise, it stops on Ben's floor. Ben and Clara are waiting, already dressed and heading out. Clara's gaze falls down my body, but she schools her expression and steps in as if she wasn't just checking me out.

"You clean up well," Ben says, joining us.

"Same." Glancing at the floor, I see that Ben is wearing his cowboy boots. "You two are leaving early," I say to pass the time on this elevator ride from hell.

How we'll all get through dinner is beyond me, though Ben seems oblivious to the tension between Clara and me. Any time he's inquired why she hasn't been down here for the past couple of years, I just told him that she's had staffing issues at work and couldn't get away.

"We were ready, so..." Ben shoots me a look over Clara's head like he's doing something wrong here. "Now all three of us can go."

"Actually, I have to go pick up my date." I dodge eye contact with Clara when she glances at me. Even when we were the best of friends, we never double-dated. I haven't been a full-time resident of Alaska since I left for college, so what time I was there, we'd spend together. I've only seen Clara with another guy a few times, but it never bothered me as much as it does right now.

Maybe it's because we're not really on speaking terms and Ben gets to talk to her all he wants. Yeah, that must be it.

"Who is it?" Ben asks as the elevator stops.

Our night doorman, Rowdy, waves to us from behind the desk.

"I was just about to call up, Mr. Greene. Your car is here." He quickly rounds the desk to open the door for us.

"Perfect," Ben says. "I was going to hitch us an Uber or taxi, but we'll just go with you."

Instinctively, I glance at Clara, and she forces a smile.

"Okay, but someone will have to sit up front once we pick up my date." My lips press together.

Ben raises his hand. "I'll take shotgun."

"Cool," I murmur, and we walk out into the San Francisco night.

It's busy for a Friday night. Couples and families are milling about, finding things to do in this amazing city I consider my second home.

At least Ben opens the vehicle door for Clara, and she slides in across the seat. It causes her dress to ride up a bit and shows off her long, tanned and toned legs. A flash of a memory of her legs sliding along mine the one night we were together assaults my mind.

"Hey, buddy," Ben says to the driver. "I'm riding shotgun with you. We have a stop to make before the restaurant."

The driver's eyebrows rise at Ben. "I'm aware, sir."

I join Clara in the back and let the two of them figure out the logistics.

Before either of them gets in the car, Clara riffles through her purse. I'm not sure whether she's actually looking for something or if she's trying to avoid my gaze.

"Who are you bringing?" she asks.

I feel like that one sentence is packed with emotions neither one of us has been able to shed since that night.

"Sessilee," I say. "She is a friend of—"

"Giulia's. I know." She nods.

Of course she does. Those two are never separated for that long in the gossip world of modeling.

"And Giulia is okay with it?" The judgment in her tone sets me back for a moment. This coming from the woman who's dating my friend and teammate after she confessed she had feelings for me two years ago?

"She should be," I half lie to both her and myself. If I wasn't so desperate, I never would've asked Sessilee. "Giulia's happily moved on. Plus, it's just dinner. Not a date. I had to find someone at the last second so your guy could get a table at a good restaurant." I bite my lip the minute I spit out how annoyed I am to be in this situation.

"Well, some men like spontaneity."

I let a low chuckle escape. "Call it what you want, but you'd probably be eating out of a food truck if it wasn't for me."

"I happen to love food trucks," she snipes.

Which I already know. We once followed a taco truck around all weekend when she came down here right before the season started years ago.

"You deserve better for a first date," I can't help but say because it's the truth.

She locks gazes with me for a beat then spits out, "Don't go pretending you know me."

The partition in the car comes down before I can respond to her ridiculous statement because I do know her. I turn and look toward the front of the car and Ben's head in the middle window.

"How you two doing back there?" he asks.

"We're good." Clara has a bright smile on now. Long gone is the scowl she wore when she was talking to me. "Just talking about Xavier bringing Sessilee to dinner."

"Sessilee? I thought you've been dodging her?" Ben says right as we pull up to the curb of the hotel she's staying at. She told me it's a short trip, that she can't stay for my game, which works out perfectly for me.

"I had to find someone." I shrug, then I think better of what I told him. "Don't tell her that."

I open the door and stand, buttoning my jacket, then walk into the hotel bar to pick her up.

Sessilee might be even more attractive than Giulia, I think, as she struts toward me wearing a hip-hugging red dress. Her long blonde hair cascades in waves down her back. She really is gorgeous, and every man in the vicinity notices as they take small glances toward her when their wives or girlfriends aren't paying attention. She grabs and holds the attention in any room.

Too bad she does nothing for me.

"Xavier," she coos when she runs her hand down my tie. "You look handsome."

"And you look beautiful. Ben and his date, Clara, are waiting in the car." I hold my arm out, and she slides her arm through mine.

"You mean *your* Clara? Ben's going out with her?"

My forehead wrinkles. "How do you know Clara?"

She giggles that fake laugh of hers. "You forget I'm your ex's best friend. Clara was her archnemesis."

Before I open the door to the car, I stop and stare at her for a moment. "Why would you say that?"

Her lips tip down at the corners. "Come on, Xavier. You can't be that clueless. You were always going on to Giulia about how upset you were that you and Clara were on the outs, and everyone knows you can't be best friends with the opposite sex. It never works out. She assumed there'd been something between you two, but I guess not if she's dating Ben."

Not wanting to get into it further, I open the door. Sessilee pretends to be thrilled to see Clara, complimenting her on her dress. Since Clara and I were already on the outs by the time I started dating Giulia, Giulia mostly ignored Clara or walked away on the rare occasion we were all together.

Sessilee's words run through my head. They're nothing new. I've been told the same thing since kindergarten when Calvin Bruns saw me playing house with Clara. "You can't be friends with a girl, Xavier." I'd asked him why and he'd shrugged and said, "It's a fact."

But I had stayed best friends with Clara all throughout my life—until that one night we crossed the line. I ache to have her back in my life. I miss my best friend. Seeing her with Ben, I can't deny that maybe Sessilee and Calvin Bruns are right. Maybe you can't be best friends with the opposite sex.

Chapter Six

Clara

We file out of the car, Xavier taking Sessilee's hand, and my stomach immediately sours. I could kick Ben in the balls for this one. I do not want to have dinner with Xavier and his perfect model date. Actually, I'm starting to regret coming here entirely, because Ben seems unsure what to do with me. I got ready an hour before we had to leave since he was watching *SportsCenter* and I was reading a book. It's like we're already an old married couple and we're not even officially a couple.

Ben wraps his arm around my waist. "Ready?"

I smile at him. "Yep."

All in all, he's not really my type of guy, but I can see he's trying—struggling, but trying.

Xavier stops at the hostess stand, and of course she fawns over the fact Xavier Greene is in the restaurant. She asks for a photo, and Xavier straightens out his suit jacket before posing for a selfie with her. That only piques the curiosity of the bystanders.

Google told me that Hillstone is the new "it" restaurant and is owned by the same chef who owns my favorite bistro two streets over. I hope that isn't the reason Xavier picked this place. I can't even explain how odd it is to be around him but act as though we're strangers.

The hostess leads us through the restaurant, and both Ben and Xavier get stopped to shake hands and say a quick hello to some patrons. The hostess glances over her shoulder as she opens the doors to the kitchen.

"And here you go. Chef's table." Her arms open wide, gesturing to an intimate table for four with candlelight and printed menus of what will be served this evening. This isn't something Xavier and I would normally do together, but I imagine he did a lot of this while dating Giulia.

"It's beautiful. You didn't have to do all this." Sessilee puts her hand over her heart and fawns over every detail, from the candlesticks to the linens.

"Thanks," Xavier says to the hostess as he slides out Sessilee's chair, but his gaze pierces mine.

How dare he give me a look to say he did this for me and not her? Irritation flares inside that I still know what his silent looks mean, but I try to push it aside.

"Here, allow me." Ben rushes to pull out my chair before I have the opportunity to do it myself.

"Thank you." I slide in, not really accustomed to this treatment. I haven't really ever been on a date this elaborate. Most men in my town think that Xavier and I are secretly sleeping together, so they don't make a move.

Once we're all seated, I look at the menu and sigh. The first appetizer is stuffed mushrooms, which I won't eat. But it's not like I'd make a big deal about it. I'm sure Ben will gladly take my portion.

Chef Ramon walks over, wiping his hands on a cloth. "Mr. Greene, it's a pleasure to serve you this evening."

Xavier stands and shakes hands with the young chef, who seems a little intimidated. "Thanks for getting us in on such short notice."

"Happy to have you. I'm really rooting for the Kingsmen

to win it this year." He looks away from Xavier to Ben. "Mr. Noughton too?"

Ben smiles and waves but doesn't stand. "Tell me you have a juicy steak you're bringing out for me." Ben holds up the menu. "This isn't going to fill me."

Chef Ramon laughs. "I'll see what I can do."

"Speaking of, can I talk to you for a moment?" Xavier steps away from the table with Chef Ramon.

"This guy took me to a restaurant once for a chef's table dinner and it was a complete nightmare. There was a fire in the kitchen, we all had to evacuate, but by the time we did, I reeked of smoke. I had to shampoo my hair five times to get the stench out. And it was a shame because the guy was hot, but I was so self-conscious after that."

I smile as nicely as possible. "That's too bad. Hopefully this one goes better."

Sessilee looks over her shoulder at Xavier. "Me and you both. I mean, Giulia will probably kill me, but I think he's worth it." She winks and shrugs.

I choke on my saliva and reach for my glass of ice water, but Ben gets a hold of it first to pass it to me. I continue having a coughing fit though, and the water spills down the front of my dress.

"Oh shit, I was trying to help you." He picks up his napkin and blots the front of my dress with his napkin.

The sound of a clearing throat interrupts us, and I look up to see Xavier's white-knuckling the back of his chair before he pulls it back. "Groping at the table might be a new thing for you, Ben." He lets out his fake laugh and sits down.

Even Sessilee shoots Xavier an inquisitive glare.

"I've got it, thanks, Ben." I take his napkin and continue blotting my dress. "It's just water. It'll dry."

Sessilee balks. "Boy, you're easygoing. I'd be throwing a

fit. That fabric is going to wrinkle before we get to the main course."

"Shit, seriously?" Ben asks, his eyes landing on my chest. "Want a blow dryer? I bet they have one in the ladies' room."

I shoo him with my hand. "I'm fine. Honestly."

"If I were you, I'd already be calling this date a disaster." Sessilee sits back at the table as a waiter comes in and pours the bottle of wine I assume Xavier ordered moments ago.

"This isn't really my scene." Ben sulks slightly.

I put my hand on his knee. Ben means well, and I already knew this isn't where he usually takes his dates. "Me either. I've never been to a chef's table."

He smiles at me, and I sense a calmness coming over him. "Not like these two." He nods toward Xavier and Sessilee.

His comment only cements the truth that Xavier and I are more different now than we've ever been.

"Since when did you two decide to team up against us?" Xavier asks, laying his napkin in his lap.

Sometimes when I see him all dressed up in a suit, so grown up from the boy I've known my entire life, he feels like a completely different person to me. A memory from the time when we were transitioning from kids to teenagers flickers in my mind.

We were thirteen and had both been invited to Kayla George's boy/girl party. It was the night before, and I was in the Greenes' basement after eating dinner. Since both of our parents had told us we had to quit sleeping over at each other's houses, my mom was due to pick me up in an hour. Xavier and I were watching a movie, some action flick he was obsessed with at the time.

I broached the subject first. "Are you nervous for tomorrow night?"

Rumors were swirling all over school that Kayla and her friends were planning on playing all the kissing games. In fact, Kayla had pulled me aside earlier that day in the girls' bathroom and asked if I'd be mad if she kissed Xavier. I told her I didn't care, Xavier could kiss who he wanted. Which was true.

"Why would I be nervous?"

I gave him a duh look. "The kissing games."

His head fell back for a moment. "You worry too much. We'll know what to do when the time comes."

We both continued to watch the movie for a moment, but I couldn't get rid of my anxiety, and I always talked to Xavier when I was anxious. He was the only one who made me feel better.

"Did you hear Tre told all the boys that Darla kissed like an open bottle? He made fun of her for not knowing how to use her tongue."

He shrugged and didn't take his eyes off the screen. "Tre's a jerk."

I had no qualms that Xavier would be polite and nice to whoever gave him his first kiss. At least, I didn't think he'd had his first kiss yet. He definitely would've told me.

"But what if I get stuck kissing someone who's experienced?"

Xavier sighed. While a female friend would've been exactly where I was emotionally with my first boy/girl party tomorrow night, Xavier was a boy, and our differences were becoming clearer the older we got.

He finally faced me, propping one leg on the couch. "You'll be fine."

I buried my head in my hands and shook it. "You say that because no girl is going to judge your kissing. They'll just be like 'I kissed Xavier and it was just the best.'" I put on my best girly-girl voice.

He chuckled. "There are plenty of experienced girls who would probably be showing me how to kiss."

"Never mind, you just don't get it." My shoulders slumped.

"I do, but... I dunno. Can't you just practice on your hand? Isn't that what girls do?"

I shrug. "I don't know, because you're my best friend and you're a guy." He laughed and I rolled my eyes and sat forward. "Forget it."

He slid closer to me on the couch and took both my hands. "Okay, sorry. What do you want me to do? Ask Fisher and Cam to come down here and show you?"

"No!" I screeched.

"Then what?"

I drew in a big breath and reminded myself that this was Xavier, my best friend. He hadn't judged me or seemed grossed out when I got my period and leaked all over the beanbag chair, while I'd been mortified and ignored him for three days. And I hadn't taken it personally when he got his first hard-on while we were watching a movie with a sex scene in it. It was just... us.

"Maybe we can practice together?" I said in a small voice.

His eyes widened. "You want to kiss me?"

I shrug. "Just for experimental reasons. Not kiss you because I like you or anything."

"Well yeah, of course not. I'm just surprised."

He contemplated for a moment because that's what Xavier did, but we were on a time crunch. My mom would be there any moment, and if we didn't kiss soon, then both of our first kisses would be tomorrow night at the party. I should have brought this up three days ago.

"It's really okay if you don't want to."

"I didn't say that." He ran his hand down the back of his head and stared at his legs for a moment. "I just don't want anything to change between us. Promise it won't." He locked his gaze with mine and I saw real fear there.

I pushed his shoulder. "Oh yeah, okay, Prince Charming. You think I'm gonna fall madly in love with you from one kiss?"

One side of his lips tipped up. "That's me, your knight in shining armor."

"Forget it." I crossed my arms.

"God, you're so stubborn." He inched forward. "Turn toward me."

"Don't be bossy."

"I'm not being bossy, but..." He glanced at the clock, and I knew as well as he did that we were close to our time being up.

I turned toward him, and we stared at one another for a beat. My heart raced when he leaned in closer, his eyes closed, and when he was about to place his lips on mine, I laughed.

"Clara," he pleaded with annoyance laced through his tone.

I straightened my back and wiggled a bit. "Sorry. Sorry. Okay, let's go again."

Xavier rolled his eyes. "Boy, does that sound appealing."

The room grew quiet, and he leaned forward again, but this time his soft lips pressed to mine, and my stomach erupted with flutters I thought would never stop. He pulled back and we stared into each other's eyes for only a second before he broke the distance again. This time he stuck his tongue in my mouth. I tried to feel sexy and comfortable as our tongues brushed against one another's, but it felt weird. Other than the butterflies in my stomach and my racing heart, I didn't see the appeal.

He drew back a second time and we both kind of shrugged. Then his hand came up to my cheek and his lips found mine a third time. And that time, heat traveled the length of my body. Our mouths seemed to get to know the other's and our tongues glided together in rhythm while a kaleidoscope of color filled my vision.

"Clara, your mom is here!" Marla called down from upstairs and we tore apart.

For a second or two, we both sat in awe. I touched my tingling lips as Xavier's chest heaved with small breaths.

"I gotta go. See you tomorrow." I grabbed my sweatshirt and ran up the stairs.

That night, for the first time ever, I understood why all the other girls looked at Xavier the way they did. But that feeling passed after a couple of minutes and he was back to just being my best friend and nothing more.

"Clara, is that okay?"

I blink, returning to the present. All three sets of eyes are on me. I look down at my plate. It's a shrimp dish covered in a sauce. Looking around, I see they all have stuffed mushrooms on their plates.

"This is great. Thank you." I look up at Chef Ramon, who I just realized has been waiting for God knows how long for me to respond.

"I'm always willing to pivot when needed. You can thank Mr. Greene for alerting me from the start. Now I'll go prepare the next dish for you all." He smiles and walks back into the kitchen area where we can watch him cook.

"Thank you," I say, my eyes landing on Xavier's fully for the first time in years.

"I know how you feel about mushrooms." He shrugs.

Sessilee laughs, but it sounds unnatural. "I feel like the third wheel. Tell me I'm not alone in this, Ben?"

Ben doesn't respond because he's eating his stuffed mushrooms. Then he shrugs one shoulder nonchalantly.

"We're just friends," I say out of habit.

"Are we?" Xavier asks, and I'm thrown off-kilter for a moment.

"There's that tension again," Sessilee comments. I'd like to shove one of the rolls in her mouth to shut her up.

I softly smile because that's all I can do right now, but I feel myself warming toward him again. I know one day I have to forgive him, if only for myself.

Chapter Seven

Xavier

*I*t's been three weeks since Clara came to San Francisco to visit Ben. Although I hated the idea of her spending the night at Ben's, I never said anything. It's not my place. I know that now. But just to be a dick, I told them to take the car I'd reserved and that I'd hitch a cab with Sessilee back to her hotel. I made sure she made it to the elevators before I turned down her invitation to join her upstairs and returned home. But Clara doesn't need to know that. Let her see how it feels. Spoiler alert—she probably doesn't care anymore.

Now it's our bye week and I decide to head to my hometown, Sunrise Bay, for two reasons. One, to see my dad, and two, to get things squared away with Clara.

Walking down the cobblestone street, I see signs in every window for the fundraiser that I had no idea was this weekend. It's an auction to raise money for the library addition.

"Xavier!"

I look to my left at The Grind and see my grandma waving. Surprisingly, she's by herself.

"Hey, Grandma." I walk over to where she sits at the outside table. "It's freezing. What are you doing out here?"

"You really became a wimp when you moved to California." She sips her steaming coffee.

I raise an eyebrow. "Thanks?"

"Sit."

I sit like a good dog because when my grandma tells me to do something, I do it.

"You're home." She smiles widely as she usually does when I return to Sunrise Bay.

"I am, just for a little bit. It's our bye week."

She nods. "I know. You think I don't follow your schedule?"

Zoe peeks her head out of The Grind. She's the owner and was my mom's best friend. They started The Grind together, and after my mom died, my dad gave it to Zoe. "X, want anything?"

I shake my head. "Nah. I'm heading to the library."

"Clara?" She smiles.

"Why else would I go?" I laugh and she does too.

"Let me grab you her usual so you can take it over. She's been working like crazy lately." The door shuts before I can say anything.

"She's been busy with the auction, I assume?"

My grandma's lips purse for a moment. "Well, since you haven't been here, let me fill you in. Gavin said there's nothing in the budget for a library extension. Gave her some five-year plan and even then, it would still be a maybe. So, she has the auction and some other fundraisers. The poor girl is fighting for something I'm not sure she'll be able to pull off. But I'm sure it keeps her from thinking of—" She sips her coffee as though she wasn't midsentence.

"Grandma?"

"Huh?"

"You were saying something."

She shakes her head. "No. I just meant the poor girl has been through so much. First her dad lost at sea, her mom dying, her grandma dying, and then, you know." She nods at me.

"Are you suggesting she lost me?" I point at my chest in disbelief. "Because she gave me up."

"I'm sure she had her reasons." She gives me a "tell me I'm wrong" expression.

I shake my head. "Has she told you something?"

She leans forward and pats my leg. "Grandmas know these things. You should talk to Cade. Hear how happy he is with Presley and now little Leighton."

I crinkle my eyebrows, trying to follow her line of thinking. Maybe her mind is going. "I have no idea what you're talking about."

She raises a shoulder and lets it drop. "It was bound to happen. You each have your own scars from that day."

My chest tightens. "I should go." I move to stand, but she pats my knee again.

"It's okay to love again. Those models you're dating." She shakes her head. "They aren't the ones for you."

"Giulia and I broke up."

"Yes, but then I saw pictures of you and another one the other day."

"That was just a dinner."

She sighs, finishes her coffee, and leaves money on the table under her mug. "Well then, you go to dinner with the wrong women."

"Great, thanks."

She shakes her head at me as though she's disappointed.

"Clara and I are—were—just friends if that's where you're going with this."

She's quick to hold up her hands in defense. "Hey, it's none of my business."

"Yet you've been harping on it since I sat down. Here I

thought maybe you just missed me." I stand and shove my hands in my pockets because damn, it's cold up here.

She steps up to me and signals for me to bend down. Once I'm in range of her hands, she presses them to my cheeks. "Everyone misses you here, but one person has been lost for some time without you. I think this trip, you need to make amends. Now, I have to go. Can you believe your brother arrested Midge?"

I don't even bother to ask why. We all know she's a klepto.

"And yet you're enjoying a cup of coffee before springing her?"

"What kind of person steals when the sheriff is in the store? They had to pretend to book her. Make it believable, you know?" She winks.

"I don't know, Fish is a by-the-book kind of guy."

"Her grandson did his engagement pictures. You're so quick to forget how things work around here." She pats my cheek and pulls me down farther to kiss it. "Love you."

"What did she steal?" I ask once I'm upright again.

She shakes her head. "A Kama Sutra book from Presley's store. She's getting more aggressive in her old age."

I chuckle. "Well, go get her out of jail."

We say our goodbyes, and I go into the store to pick up Clara's drink from the counter and leave a tip for Zoe before sneaking out the back door. A few minutes later, I'm staring at the library and working up the nerve to enter.

"Here goes nothing."

"I'M REALLY BUSY. I can't talk right now."

Those were Clara's words yesterday. She said she'd call

me, but she didn't. She's been stubborn her whole life, but I never knew she could be *this* stubborn. I left the library, not wanting to push it and make a scene at her workplace, but I grabbed a flyer for the auction.

Now I'm seated in a plastic chair, having to put on a fake smile in front of all the townspeople.

"Is there a bachelor auction or something I don't know about tonight?" Mandi, my stepsister, sits down next to me.

"Funny." I roll my eyes.

"I'm serious. They'd get good coin for you. Maybe then Clara will forgive you for whatever you've done."

From my knowledge, the only ones who know what went down with us are Presley and Cade.

"How do you know it was me?"

She tilts her head and gives me that coy smirk that says she's not stupid.

"Whatever."

"Then why are you here?" Mandi asks, fiddling with her phone.

"To try to get a few minutes alone with Clara."

"Ha. Good luck with that. That girl has skipped all our girls' nights out lately because of work and all this fundraising she's trying to put together for the library."

I look around the room and it's mostly townspeople here. Who is gonna buy something at an auction when they could just give the money to Clara? "What did you donate?"

"A weekend stay at the inn." Mandi shrugs. "Not sure who'd buy it though."

"Maybe someone will buy it for a family member."

"Maybe."

The clearing of a throat through a microphone grabs our attention. Clara stands at the front of the room. "Hi, for those of you who don't know me, I'm Clara Harrison, the librarian for our library here in Sunrise Bay."

"Please, girl, I've known you since you had a gap in your teeth," a woman shouts from a few rows back.

I smile, remembering that little girl from kindergarten who came up to me on the playground and asked to throw the football with me. Out of all the kids, she somehow picked me to be friends with.

Clara smiles. "Hello, Miss Polly... I want to thank everyone for joining us tonight and let you know that all money collected tonight is going toward an expansion to the library. So, let's get started and happy bidding."

"Let's go, Dori!" Grandma rushes in and beelines it right to the front row.

Dori makes her way up the aisle at a leisurely pace as though she hasn't got anywhere to be.

When Grandma reaches the front row, she shoos a couple there. "You people without cataracts belong in the back."

The couple looks at one another and slides into the row behind us.

"Only her," I mumble to Mandi.

"Definitely."

Once the two grandmas are situated, Clara brings up the first item—a complete makeover at Fringe, donated by my other stepsister, Posey. Then there's a beer named after someone from my brother Cade and stepbrother Jed. A flower arrangement class from Twisted Stem, a toolbox from Handyman Haven, a glass blowing class by Fired Up, and of course Mandi's weekend getaway.

"Thanks for your generosity, everyone. This is going great." Clara's appreciative smile shines over the room. Her blonde hair is twisted into some sort of updo that elongates her neck, and the deep *V* of her dress makes me remember the valley between her breasts. The way her back arched off the bed as I took her nipple in my mouth.

I clear my throat and shift in my seat. I shouldn't be thinking about that. I'm here to get Clara back in my life as a *friend*.

"For our next item, we've been donated something extremely unique and special. To explain each item in better detail than I could, let me bring up the talented man responsible."

"Shut up," Mandi murmurs next to me.

"What?"

"Everyone, this is Noah," Clara says.

"As in our nephew?" I laugh, but Mandi doesn't. Her eyes are on the man walking up the aisle. He's huge, his dark hair pulled back into a ponytail, and has a beard. He could be one of my tackles. "Who's he?"

"Midge's grandson."

"And we like Midge's grandson?"

She turns my way finally and blushes.

"Do we like Midge's grandson?"

"Shut up, Xavier. We don't. He's just... he just spends some time at the inn on occasion."

"Okay." I think there's a lot more I'm missing, but Mandi has never shared a lot of her love life with the boys in the family. Since I don't want her to call out my own shit, I let the topic go.

Noah goes to the podium and Clara stands a little too close to him if you ask me. He picks up a framed photo and places it on an easel. "This is a picture of a moose lying down with the mountains behind it."

And that's not all he's got. For the next fifteen minutes, Clara auctions off photos of a bald eagle with wings spread, flying in the air, a bear and her cub fishing for salmon in a river, wolf packs, and sea lions. All while Noah explains where and how he got each shot.

"The man is talented," I mumble. I'd seen the family photos he did for Fisher and Ally, but this is the first time I've seen any of his wildlife pictures.

"Yeah, he is."

"I wonder if he's as talented in other areas." I waggle my eyebrows, and Mandi elbows me hard.

Clara steps back up to the podium. "Okay, that's all for tonight. I can't thank—"

"Nope. I have my own donation." Grandma stands.

Mandi and I share a look because this can't be good. I don't know exactly what *this* is, but I know it's not good—for someone.

"Oh, Ethel, I didn't know. I'm sorry. What is it?" Clara, always the polite one.

Grandma looks around the room until her gaze stays on me.

"Shit," I say under my breath.

"My grandson, Xavier. A dinner with him. He's the quarterback of the Kingsmen down in San Francisco. Come on, ladies. Now's your chance."

"Um... Grandma? May I?"

"Don't be shy. Come on up and let them get a good look," she says.

I look at Mandi, who can't bite her lip hard enough to stop from laughing.

"Thanks for the help." I stand and walk down the aisle.

"This is unusual, but let's go with it. How about we start bidding at five dollars?" Clara says with the gavel in her hand, ready to point.

"Five dollars?" My forehead wrinkles.

"I've got ten."

Clara points at a girl we went to high school with, then covers the microphone with her hand and says, "Stop complaining, your price is already going up."

The bidding continues, and I'll admit it feels good to be so wanted.

Then Dori, my grandma's blue-haired best friend, raises her hand. "One thousand."

"Whoa!" Clara points at her. "You're the winner!"

"Isn't there, like, a three-second countdown or something?" I ask.

"Nah, a thousand dollars is a big deal here, or have you forgotten?" Her sneer doesn't go unnoticed.

I step down and walk over to the elderly lady. "Thank you, Dori. I have some bad news though. I only have this weekend available. Then I have to go back to San Francisco."

"Perfect, let's do it tomorrow night."

Clara comes down and hugs Dori, thanking her for such a big donation.

"Oh please, with this heartthrob, I would've paid more. I got a steal."

Just like my Friday nights back home, my evening is now booked with a date—with Dori Bailey.

Chapter Eight

Clara

I cannot believe no one was available to take a picture of Xavier and Dori enjoying dinner together. My plan is to get pictures of each of the winners enjoying their prize to help with further fundraising down the road. Just a simple shot with a cell phone would've sufficed. I even asked Ethel, and she went on and on about how she can't figure out these new cell phones for the life of her.

So as I walk into Northern Lights Retirement Center, I'm prepared for an ambush. I've seen every Greene sibling get manipulated by the grandmas and I'm not naive enough to think they don't have a plan. I'm fully prepared to be locked in a closet or something with Xavier.

"Hi, LeeAnn," I say to the receptionist.

"Oh." She bolts up from her seat. "Ethel mentioned you'd be by."

I hold up my phone. "I'm only here to snap a picture really quick, then I'll be on my way. Do you happen to know if they're going out somewhere or are they having dinner here?"

"Um…" She looks down the hall toward the main entertaining area. "I'm not sure. Why don't you wait right here? I'll be right back."

"Really, it'll only take a moment." I saw Xavier's truck that he leaves at his house up here and Dori's Cadillac that she never drives out front.

But LeeAnn disappears around the corner, so I lean my hip on the desk and stare at brochures about what a wonderful place Northern Lights Retirement is.

"You can't do that, Grandma!" Xavier's voice echoes through the empty hallway in the opposite direction from where LeeAnn went. He's probably in his grandma's room, but I can't see him because they're around the corner. "You can't just connive your way into us making up, though I wish you could."

"You're kidding me, right? You've had two years. She was your best friend and don't pretend you don't want her back. Everyone in town knows you do."

"Mind your own business. All of you. I'll send you back the thousand dollars Dori donated." He turns the corner and stops when he sees me standing there.

"Xavier," Ethel snipes, lagging behind. I've only ever heard that stern tone in her voice a few times.

He throws his hands in the air. "What do you want from me?"

Ethel comes into view and glances in my direction. "Clara." Her voice full of sugar.

"I... um..." I feel uncomfortable having overheard their conversation.

Xavier lowers his head and his chest heaves with a deep breath.

"Oh, the picture. Surely you can stick around for a picture, right?" She touches Xavier's arm. "Right?"

He looks up and locks eyes with me. "Yeah, I'll take the picture. I don't want to ruin it for you, Clara."

"Great! Dori!" Ethel yells.

"I'm right here," Dori says, coming from around the same corner.

"Perfect. Let's get going then." Ethel hikes her purse farther up her shoulder.

"I thought we were having dinner here?" Xavier asks.

"Can you just pose in the lobby here?" I motion toward the open area at my back. "That will suffice."

"No. No." Ethel waves off my suggestion. "Dori secured reservations at her grandson's fancy restaurant in Lake Starlight."

"But I don't need to..." I stop because a fight you know you're not going to win isn't worth it.

"Clara can take the picture here," Xavier says. "Why can't we just do that?"

"Because"—Ethel eyes Xavier—"Dori paid the most money out of anyone at the auction and if you take the picture at her grandson's restaurant, it drives in some business there. You'd be helping him."

Dori's face lights up. "That's true. He just told me the other day that the restaurant has been struggling a little. Do you know how many kids he has?"

Xavier shrugs. "Like, ten?"

"Five. But he has two who are going to college soon." Dori looks between Xavier and me with pleading eyes.

I'm not going to be a bitch to some old lady. "Okay, I'll follow you all there. What's the restaurant called?"

"Parking is hard to find because it's right in the middle of downtown, so how about Xavier just drives us all?" Dori suggests.

Ethel's face lights up. "Yes, I've been waiting for a ride in that truck of yours."

"Why?" Xavier asks. Clearly he's going to continue to be difficult.

"What am I going to do while you guys are having dinner if I'm stuck there?" I ask.

Ethel pats my arm. "We can have some girl time. I was thinking about getting a tattoo and Dori's granddaughter married Liam Kelly, who owns Smokin' Guns Tattoo Shop."

Okay well, I can't let that happen. "Or maybe we just walk around the square," I suggest.

"I'd like that. I can tell you stories about your grandmother. She was one of my best friends, you know."

"I know." I smile at her, remembering how Ethel took me under her wing as a pseudo granddaughter after mine died. This is the least I can do. "Okay, let's go."

"You realize they're gonna lock us in a closet somewhere or something?" Xavier asks me on the way outside.

I tilt my head side to side. "We'll be in public. They lose all their control once they're out of these walls."

Xavier shakes his head. "You underestimate their level of scheming."

When we reach his truck, I go to the back, but Ethel insists I sit in front. The restaurant is only fifteen minutes away.

Lake Starlight is so pretty no matter what time of year it is. The sidewalk is lined with trees lit with string lights, and there're all kinds of small custom shops I'm sure the tourists love.

Xavier slams on the brakes when we start past the town square, and I jolt forward.

"You have two old ladies back here!" Ethel scolds.

He rolls down his window. "Rylan, whatcha doing?"

I lean forward to see past him and find the youngest Greene, Rylan, with Dori's first great-grandchild, Calista Bailey. They're sitting hand in hand in the gazebo in the middle of the square and Rylan just waves with this free hand in response to his brother.

"Aren't they so cute?" Dori says. "We didn't have to work our magic with those two at all. It's like it's destiny."

"We better go chaperone." Ethel opens her door. "We'll meet you at the restaurant. Terra and Mare. Right there with the burgundy awning." She points just ahead and on the right before she and Dori exit the truck.

"I always thought they didn't like each other," I say as he drives off.

Xavier rolls his eyes. "So did I. Still think the grandmas' intentions are pure?" He parks in a spot right outside Terra and Mare.

"They'll be back soon, but I can't believe little Ryguy has a girlfriend." I admire them for a moment before Xavier clears his throat and I turn to see that he's holding open the restaurant door for me.

I walk through and a man is standing there waiting for us. He's wearing a chef's jacket, but I've seen Rome Bailey, the owner of the restaurant, and this isn't him.

"I'm Chef Colin. I'll be serving you tonight." He holds out his hand and we each shake it in turn and introduce ourselves.

A minute later, we hear a key in a lock. Xavier turns to the door, walks over, and tries to open it, but it's been locked from the outside.

"Back door?" Xavier asks Chef Colin without sounding as though he has much hope.

"Sorry, locked. I could let you out of course, but then I'd have to deal with Dori and Ethel, and to be honest with you, they kind of scare me." He cringes. "So, it's just the three of us tonight. Please have a seat and I'll bring out a bottle of wine for you to enjoy." He disappears into the kitchen.

We both look at the candlelit table for two.

"Goddamn. Why can't they mind their business?" Xavier pushes his hands through his dark-blond hair.

I step over to the table. "Because they're Dori and Ethel."

"Just wait." He comes up alongside me and pulls out my chair. "This is you making the most of it?"

I shrug. "Yep. We're not getting out of here until dinner is over. We don't have to discuss anything we don't want to. We can just sit and enjoy dinner in silence for all I care. I'll snap a picture of you and Dori afterward."

Lie. Being in Xavier's presence again these past few days has me missing his company more than I have in a long time.

I slide into my seat, and he tucks in my chair.

"I suppose." He sits down across from me, and we both put our napkins in our laps. After that, Xavier relaxes back in his seat, one arm stretched across the table. "How's Ben?"

"Next topic."

Chef Colin comes out, and we don't say anything while he fills our glasses with merlot. He's quick to leave, probably sensing the tension in the air.

"Why can't we talk about Ben?"

"Because it's uncomfortable." I sip my wine, hoping he'll drop it.

"Okay then, how about the fundraiser? I'd love to contribute a large sum of money to get you closer to your goal."

I shake my head. "I don't want you to swoop in as the savior. The town will benefit from the addition. I'm confident we can raise enough money."

"I'd pay for the whole thing if you let me." He winks.

Prior to the past few years, Xavier was never one to throw around his money. Sure, he tried so many times to pay my student loans or buy me a new car, but he was never flashy the way he was when he was up here with Giulia.

It doesn't matter though. His money is not what I wanted from our friendship. He's given me comfort, companionship, and stability over the years, but the one thing I ended up needing from him the most, he was unable to give me.

"Stop. I don't want your money."

"The money is for the town."

"X, enough."

He stares at me and the candlelight flickers in his hazel eyes.

"What?" I ask.

"I miss you calling me X. I miss *you*, Clara."

I shake my head. "I'm not ready to talk about this."

"Come on, it's been over two years."

I look outside, and even with the drapes drawn, I spot Rylan and Calista eating ice cream with no Dori or Ethel in sight. Young love. Maybe that's all this is with Xavier, even if I'm not young anymore. Maybe the seed was planted when I was young. He probably filled some void when I'd lost everyone in my life, and I've confused what's between us for love.

"I'd just rather forget it," I mumble.

"I can do that."

I huff because of course he's willing to forget it, he was in the wrong. "You're really okay with me and Ben?"

He shrugs one shoulder and stares into his wineglass. "It's sort of weird, but if he's who you want... plus, he hasn't been out with anyone else, so he must be pretty into you. Which I think I knew would happen."

I know this conversation is making him uncomfortable because he's looking at his hand and playing with the tablecloth.

"Why would you say that?"

His movements freeze and his gaze flicks in my direction.

We're interrupted by Chef Colin placing bowls of soup in front of us. Lobster bisque. After we say our thanks, he nods and heads back into the kitchen.

"Any guy would be lucky to have your heart. Of course he'd fall for you," he says softly.

"Just not you." The words slide out of me before I can catch them. "Forget it."

He leans in closer to me over the table. "It's not what you think. I just know I'd end up hurting you. You know my feelings on forever, Clara. I don't want a family. My job doesn't afford me the luxury."

I tilt my head because there are plenty of professional athletes with wives and kids.

"Okay, some people make that work. But think about what you really want, Clara. Do you want a relationship with a guy who lives so far away, you need a plane ticket to see him? You're not leaving Alaska permanently. Even if you did, would you want to be with someone who might have to move every few years if he gets traded? Not to mention the football groupies and the media and constant travel for away games. I can't offer stability, and you deserve that."

"You don't have to tell me all the reasons you think you can't have a real relationship, but what I find funny is that you had one with Giulia." I can't help the bitterness that coats my words.

He scowls. "You think we had a relationship? Half the time she was in Europe, modeling. She rarely came to my games. And I was good with that. But that's not what you deserve."

The more he talks, the angrier I become. "Stop acting

like you're not good enough for me." I down the rest of my wine.

"It's the truth. I won't do that to you."

"I'm not some fragile piece of china, Xavier. Yes, we slept together, and I had hopes that it would turn into more, but what did you do? You ignored everything that night meant to the both of us. Do you think you can mask that you felt the same way in the moment? God, Xavier, neither of us were that drunk. Really think back to that night. That wasn't a one-night stand with a friend. I figured you needed time to realize giving us a go might be a good thing. But then one of your friends shows interest and you tell him he can't? It's like you were putting me on the shelf in case you wanted to come back and play with me."

"It was fresh. I was so fucking confused. And I'm allowing you to date him now, so stop being pissy with me."

I double blink. "You're *allowing* me?" I raise my eyebrows and wait for him to say something else.

"You know what I mean."

I release a deep breath and stare out the window. I'm so tired of fighting with him. So tired of carrying around this animosity. I just have to accept that he won't ever feel the same way for me as I do for him. I can't fault him for it. He may have been high handed in the way he handled everything but is the satisfaction of punishing him really worth losing my best friend for any longer than I already have?

"I'm fucking this all up. I just want you back in my life. I miss you." He slides his chair around so he's next to me. "I miss you so fucking bad, Clara."

"As a friend?"

His face drops and his hazel eyes have a sheen on them. "I wish I could give you what you want."

"I'm not sure I want that from you at this point anyway. I

mean, I did two years ago, but now?" I shake my head. I love him so much, but I'm not going to beg a guy to love me or drag him into a relationship and have him resent me in the long run.

"Oh."

Chef Colin comes out and stops. "You've barely touched your soups and I have your salads."

"Can you give us ten minutes?" Xavier asks, then returns his attention to me.

Chef Colin nods then leaves.

"I'm sorry for crossing that line with you two years ago when I wasn't ready for us to be more than friends. It was a shit thing to do to you. And I'm sorry for telling Ben he couldn't date you. That was a dick move after I'd made it clear I didn't want us to date. I'm also sorry for rubbing Giulia in your face and bringing her here. I was really messed up when you stopped talking to me. Everything I did, I did in an effort to keep things the same between us because I never wanted to lose you, but it all backfired and I ended up losing you anyway. I'll do whatever you need me to in order to get our friendship back, just say the word. But please forgive me." His hand slides into mine and his warmth travels up my arm.

There's no denying that this man feels like home to me. Maybe we are only meant to be friends. I can accept that. But I can't accept not having the man I used to trust more than anyone in this world not be in my life anymore.

I nod.

"Really?" A half smile forms on his face like he doesn't want to get his hopes up.

I nod again.

He whoops and beams, standing and pulling me to my feet and right into his arms. I forgot how good it feels to have him wrapped around me, and I inhale the scent of his cologne. But the musky citrus smell only spurs a memory from our night together. Surely I can get past the feeling of wanting him as more than a friend. I have to if I want to go back to the way things were before.

Two hours later, after Xavier and I have talked and laughed over dinner the way we used to, the front door unlocks and in walks Rome Bailey.

He shakes his head but has a smile. "I'm sorry, you two. I was out of town with my wife for a getaway. I had no idea the two grandmas convinced Colin to open up on a day we're usually closed."

We both stand and shake his hand, complimenting him on the restaurant.

"I heard they even enlisted Rylan and Calista." He shakes his head. "You two kiss and make up?"

"Oh no." I shake my head. "We're just friends. They wanted us to become friends again."

He smirks. "You should talk to my sister, Juno. She had a guy best friend once too."

"What happened?" Xavier asks.

Rome puts his hand on Xavier's shoulder. "He's her husband now. Good luck, you two. Now excuse me while I go talk to Colin." He disappears into the kitchen.

Rylan walks in seconds later. "Can we go now?"

"Where's Calista?" Xavier asks.

His face distorts. "I don't know. Grandma paid us to pretend we were dating."

Xavier looks at me. "Not so innocent, are they?"

"I guess you were right this time."

He puts his arm around my shoulders. "I'll take it."

I can't deny it feels good to be friends with him again. I just hope my heart remembers that's all it will ever be.

Chapter Nine

Xavier

I can't believe she's forgiven me. After two years, it finally feels as if some of the weight I was carrying around on my shoulders has lifted.

But it's still a little awkward. Since I only have two more days here, I asked Clara to Truth or Dare for lunch, wanting to speed up this process of being comfortable with each other so we can move back into our best-friends status.

Stopping by the library to pick her up, I find Unessa behind the desk.

Her lips press together when she looks up from what she's doing and sees me. "Oh, Mr. Quarterback is back in town."

"Hi, Unessa." She's a few years younger than me and I swear she plots my death a new way every time I see her. I don't know if she's party to what went down between Clara and me, or if she just hates me. "Is Clara here?"

She tucks a piece of her purple hair behind her ear and continues to scan in some books.

"Unessa. Clara?"

She looks up at me again with a bored expression. "She's in the romance section. Don't go reading into that and run off now." She points as if I don't know the way. I helped Clara reorganize that section four years ago.

"Always a pleasure." I nod and leave her to her scanning.

But a kid comes up right after me and she makes him recite the alphabet before she'll help him locate the book he wants. The kid is, like, seven, but she tells him she can't just hand him everything without him having to work for it like some people. I'm pretty sure she's looking in my direction with that reference.

Forgetting Unessa, I walk through the library and so many memories surface, but it's the one from four years ago that I can see as clear as glass.

Clara had to move romance to a bigger section because it was becoming so popular with the patrons, and they were carrying more and more titles. It was early summer, so I was still in off-season and had reserved the entire weekend to help her. The only problem was that the air conditioner in the library had broken down and no one could come to help until the following week, even when I bribed them. That's life in a small town though. You get used to that kinda thing.

"I feel like all this should be in a curtained-off section with a warning like the video stores used to have for pornos." I picked up Charmed by the Bartender *by Piper Rayne and read the dedication that said it was written for all the ladies looking for their very own unicorn cock then turned to Clara. "Do I want to know what a unicorn cock is?"*

She laughed. "Use your imagination, X, and will you please stop reading the books and come help me actually put them in order?"

She blew her brown hair out of her face, and I watched a drop of sweat disappear down the valley between her breasts. I stilled for a moment, confused about what that twitch of my cock meant. Sure, there'd been times I'd seen Clara in a bikini or that time when we got caught in the rain and she had to wear my clothes while hers dried, and I remember feeling attracted to her then. But I always pushed the feeling down. I couldn't lust after Clara.

I picked up the book a couple down from the one I'd just had in my hand. "Here's another one from the same series. Women really like this, huh?" I read the passage to her in my most breathy voice.

"Mr. Banks, would you like me to take care of these pants for you? My hand snakes down his muscular chest until I cup his balls in my palm, squeezing and massaging.

"I'd like you to do that on your knees, Miss Hart." He cocks his eyebrow as though he's daring me.

Does he not get me at all? A dare pretty much guarantees I'm going to do whatever it is. I enjoy a challenge.

I sink to my knees, staring up at him as I swiftly unbutton his charcoal slacks." I roll my eyes. "I mean, really?"

Clara sat back on the chair with a pile of books in her lap and stared at me for a moment. "Does it not turn you on?"

I shrugged. "Maybe I'm a visual guy. I need to see it play out on a screen."

"You honestly can't use your imagination? Come on." She picked up another book and read an excerpt that flushed my cheeks, but still, I was more uncomfortable than I was aroused. "Nothing?"

"Give me porn over this any day."

"That's just lazy." She shuffled through a few books.

Either it was growing hotter in there or I was actually turned on. Her chest shined with moisture, and for the very first time in my life, I wondered what it would be like to sleep with Clara. Okay, not the very first time. She'd been my best friend through all of puberty. But this time, I actually visualized it. Her underneath me, sweat coating both of us from fucking so hard we could barely catch our breaths.

"Shut your eyes," she said.

"This is ridiculous. You women can have your romance books and the guys will stick to porn."

"Do you know how unrealistic porn is? I read this article about how boys watch porn since it's so accessible now, then they think that's what women want—to be strangled or slapped on the ass or told they're a dirty slut. I mean sure, some women do like that, but I don't think a young girl exploring her first sexual encounter is ready for that kind of thing. That's more something you lean into once you've had some sexual experience and you know what you like, what you want to explore, what makes you feel fulfilled and gratified. Talk about throwing someone in the deep end of the pool who can't swim."

I laughed. "I think you're being a little dramatic."

"I'm not. I swear. You should check in with Rylan before he hits those years. You don't want him experiencing his first time and thinking he needs to shove a cucumber up the poor girl's ass or something."

"Clara, what the fuck?" I'd never heard her talk like that before, and damn it all to hell if I wasn't turned on. Not because I wanted to shove a cucumber anywhere, but all this talk about sex had made me horny.

"Just close your eyes for a moment. Let me read you something. Free your mind and just let your imagination run wild. Okay?"

I shut my eyes because I knew Clara well enough, she was stubborn as hell and this wouldn't end until I did what she wanted.

"So beautiful," he murmurs, his knuckles gliding along the swell of my breast. 'I almost don't want to unwrap you.

It's then that I witness Dean taking me in like a piece of precious art he's waited decades to view. His tongue slides out and he licks his bottom lip.

While he admires me, I pull his shirt from his body, letting it join his jacket on the floor. I look at a man five years older, more muscled, more defined. We've grown. His flat stomach now has more dark hair trickling down past his waistband, his nipples more prominent on stronger pecs. He's turned from boy to man, and I missed the transformation.

"Dean?" I break up the mood. Not that I'm not enjoying what he's doing, but Dean doesn't do gentle caressing.

"Uh-huh," he murmurs, his lips touching my skin and finding their way down to my breasts.

"Don't treat me like I'm damaged goods." He lifts his head and stares at me like I'm a crossword clue he can't figure out.

"What?"

"You don't need to be gentle with me just to prove you've changed."

The one side of his lips lift. He knows exactly what I'm referring to. Our sex life was never tame—it was break the table, shatter the lamp kind of sex.

"Are you asking me to fuck you, Chelsea Walsh?" A full smile creases his lips, his forefingers and thumbs now pinching my nipples harder. A moan falls from my lips.

One hand covers my right breast, and he squeezes and then massages it. The fine art of hard and soothing—no one knows it better than him. He bends down, taking my nipple into his mouth as his arm slides under my back along the counter. In one motion, he pulls me up to him. My legs wrap around his torso so that he doesn't have to stop tormenting me with small bites to my pebbled nipples while he carries me to the living room.

"Place your hands on the couch, gorgeous." His voice

transforms to that authoritative mix of stern and sultry that I love.

I do as he says, my ass out for his viewing pleasure. One hand smacks my ass and then slides down, gripping and squeezing.

Then my body ignites with the sound of his belt being unbuckled and the thud as it falls to the floor, along with his pants.

"I'm torn on having you strip me down the rest of the way, or me bending you over and hammering into you." I close my eyes as shivers rush across my skin.

Fuck. Hearing Clara read that sample made me want to have her read me more—preferably while we're naked in bed.

"So?" she asked.

"I get it. It's hot, but romance novels aren't as realistic as pornography. Men aren't heroes who know what a woman wants right away. They aren't mind readers."

Clara laughed and held up a bunch of books. "Exactly. Long live the book boyfriend. But you don't think any women in porn have ever faked it?" She arched an eyebrow.

I sat in the chair next to her, hoping it would somehow cool me down.

"But I think you're wrong, Xavier, just so you know."

"Wrong about what?" I organized the authors with last names beginning with R on the table in front of us.

"There are a lot of guys in real life who are like book boyfriends. Sure, it's not as exaggerated like in books, but there are men who are there for the love of their life when they need them the most. The ones who hold them when they've had a bad day and cheer from the sidelines when they accomplish a goal. Just look at you."

My face scrunched up as though I'd smelled something off-putting. "What about me?"

"You're a football star from a small town. You're kind to elders, treat women with respect, give to charities. I know you don't want to hear it, but you'll make a great husband someday. And a father too. One who's more than worthy to be written into a romance book. I can't speak on the sex though. You might be lousy in bed." Her head rocked back in laughter, and something overcame me when I saw her elongated neck. All I envisioned was my tongue sliding up past her chin and devouring her mouth.

"Guess you'll never know." My voice cracked a bit.

She sobered and her head came back down. "Guess not."

Our eyes locked for a long moment, and the heat already filling the small area intensified and grew heavier.

"Would you want to know?" I asked, leaning toward her, as though I couldn't help myself and was drawn to her by some force stronger than myself.

"I don't know. I mean..." Her voice was as soft as silk.

"Clara..."

Somehow, she knew that in that moment that her name on my lips was me asking for permission to kiss her. Her tongue came out and she licked her lips, granting me a small nod.

I moved forward and she moved toward me. Everything in me told me it was wrong, but it was as if I had no control over my motions. The next thing I knew, my hand was on her neck, my thumb running down the center, pulling her to me. Our lips were millimeters apart when a loud sound echoed through the room.

We both jumped back to find Art, the janitor, walking in with two large fans. "Thought you two might need these at least. It's as hot as a sauna in here."

Clara got to her feet. "Thank you so much, Art."

"No problem. Romance section, huh?" His bushy gray eyebrows raised, and he walked away. "I'll lock up on my way out."

"Thanks, Art." Clara turned toward me for a beat as if she

wanted to say something, then turned back to the table to organize the books.

We finished the new romance section and the almost kiss was never talked about again.

"Oh, you're early," Clara says, drawing my mind from the memories.

"Yeah, sorry."

She smiles like the Clara I've always known, but it's still not quite as easygoing as it used to be. That'll take time, I'm sure.

I match her smile. "I can wait if you're not ready."

She chuckles. "Not in this section. We don't need you reading any more excerpts."

So I'm not the only one who remembers that night.

We walk out of the library, and I squint at the bright sun. We walk over to Truth or Dare, chatting about nothing of importance.

I'm about to open the door to the brewery when a voice calls, "Clara!"

I know that voice, so it's no surprise to me that when I turn, I find Ben jogging down the cobblestone path with his suitcase bouncing along behind him.

I've never been more disappointed to see one of my friends in my life.

Chapter Ten

Clara

"**B**en?" I have to be seeing things. Why on earth is Ben in Sunrise Bay?

"X? What's up?" He stops short and does a whole handshake thing with Xavier before we do the do we or don't we hug awkward dance. Finally, he does the pat on my back semihug thing.

I wish my feelings for Ben were stronger. And I really wish I was excited to see him, rather than the disappointment I feel because of what him being here means for my lunch with Xavier.

"What are you doing here?" I ask.

Ben smiles that boy-next-door smile that could win the heart of any girl. Any girl except me, because there's another boy next door I gave my heart to a long time ago. "We have a bye week, and I was sitting alone in my condo, and I just thought... why not surprise Clara?" His smile falters. "It's okay, right?"

"Of course. We were just about to have lunch, come on." I open the door of the brewery and walk in.

"Maybe I should let the two of you catch up?" Xavier says when we walk in.

"Nah, come on." Ben clasps him on the shoulder and we head to an available table.

Molly walks over. Her belly isn't really showing yet, but then again, she's wearing a sweatshirt. She places the menus on the table. "Look who's back in town."

"What are you doing here?" I ask.

She sighs. "We've been short staffed and I've had to come in to cover shifts here and there."

"How are you feeling?" It's hard not to notice how tired she looks.

Her head sways left then right. "The nausea is getting better thank God, but now we have a jealous little girl at home."

"Emelia is jealous?" Xavier asks, concern in his tone.

"Afraid so. She doesn't like Jed giving my stomach any attention. Every time he uses the phrase 'when the baby comes,' she changes the subject. I have to find a way for her to bond before the baby is born."

"Mind if I stop by later?" Xavier asks.

"You're always welcome. Why?"

Xavier shrugs. "Something I need to talk to my niece about."

Molly shoots him an expression of appreciation, then moves her gaze around the table. "Okay, what can I get you all?"

I order an iced tea, Xavier orders a water, and Ben orders Lucy's Flight.

After Molly's gone, the table is quiet, and I search my mind for something to talk about and settle on the weather. How lame.

"How is the weather in San Francisco?"

"Foggy," Xavier says at the same time Ben says, "Rainy."

I concentrate on the menu as though I don't know by heart everything they serve here. Awkward doesn't even come close to describing this situation.

"I thought Coach wanted you in San Francisco today?" Ben asks Xavier, and I tilt my head.

"I told him I need a few mental health days." Xavier doesn't look up from the menu. "He doesn't have to worry about me."

What the hell are they talking about?

"Is something wrong?" I ask.

"No. My knee took a beating last Sunday, so Coach wants me with the trainers, but it's fine."

The pit in my stomach says Xavier isn't feeling one hundred percent physically. I'm shocked he's going against his coach's wishes. That's not like him at all.

"So where are you staying?" Xavier asks Ben.

Ben looks my way. I suppose I should offer to repay the favor of him letting me stay at his place when I went to visit him.

"Oh. I have more than enough room," I say.

Xavier clears his throat, and before Molly even gets a chance to put down his water, he takes it from her and gulps a large swig.

"Great," Ben says. "I'm only here until Sunday. We have practice on Monday, so I have to be back for that. I did some research on the plane and there's a restaurant in a neighboring town called Terra and Mare. It's supposed to be the fanciest one around here, so I made us reservations for tonight."

My eyes catch Xavier's across the table. One side of his lips tips up as though he's happy we were already there yesterday. As if this is a game we're playing. Arrogance shines bright on him, and I can't quite determine what that means.

Molly returns to the table, and we order our lunch.

Xavier has his usual quesadilla, me a BLT, and Ben orders a quesadilla and a burger with fried pickles.

"And another flight," Ben says, raising his hand to her before she leaves. "It was a bumpy flight and I'm not the best flyer."

I almost spit out my iced tea. "Really?"

"Why do you find that so funny?" Ben looks offended, so I extend my hand across the table to touch his forearm.

"I'm sorry. I didn't mean it like that. You're just... you're a big guy and I can't picture you scared of anything."

"Oh, Ben's scared of plenty." Xavier smiles over the rim of his water. "Is that more like date five material, or are you going to tell her now? Maybe just get it out of the way."

"It's, like, after marriage material, but..."

I lean back in my chair, waiting for Ben to enlighten me.

"Spiders for one." Ben's body racks in shivers.

Xavier and I laugh, our eyes catching across the table for a moment. That nonverbal language between us alive and well once again.

"Heights. Which accounts for the whole airplane thing. And I absolutely hate any being that flies."

"That's not that bad." I smile across the table at Ben.

"Wait until you see a pigeon fly at him." Xavier laughs. "Flails like a little girl."

Ben shakes his head and finishes off another one of the beers on his flight.

I point at Xavier. "Let's remember who ran out of that haunted house screaming when we were nine."

Xavier shudders. "I told you a ghost grabbed my arm."

I playfully roll my eyes. "Likely story."

"And you're always making fun of me?" Ben asks Xavier, shaking his head.

"You're the Hulk. It's funny that you're always scared of stuff."

Molly brings our food over and we all eat. The awkwardness from earlier eases and it just feels like three friends getting together and making conversation.

"How long have you two been friends?" Ben asks.

We both look up from our meals. "Kindergarten," we answer in unison.

"Seriously? I don't even remember the names of the kids I went to elementary school with, let alone still talk to them. But it must help with the trust issues you have." He elbows Xavier.

I tilt my head, and Xavier peers up through his thick eyelashes for a beat before looking back down at his plate.

"You have a big mouth," he murmurs and takes a bite of his quesadilla.

"I thought you two weren't just friends, you were best friends? She doesn't know about that?" Ben takes a big bite out of his burger.

"There are some things only other players understand." Xavier shoots him a look as though he's telling Ben to shut the fuck up.

But Ben doesn't seem to clue in. "You know the women who only want us for our status and money? Scares Xavier."

He's never discussed that with me. I wish it didn't feel like a dagger to the heart. I've always told him everything.

"Mind your own business, Ben." Xavier looks across the restaurant. "Jed!"

Jed, his stepbrother, walks over and turns the empty chair beside me around, straddling it. "What's up? I heard you were back in town for a bit."

"Yeah, I'm picking up Dad from treatment." Xavier lifts

his wrist to check his watch. I recognize it as being from the watch company he does ads for.

"He's doing great from what Mom says." Jed looks from me to Xavier and back to me. Jed's never been subtle, and he wags a finger between the two of us. "What's with you two being at the same table?"

I look at Xavier to answer the question and he shrugs a shoulder. "We made up."

"You were fighting?" Ben looks at Xavier in confusion.

Molly arrives with the next flight for Ben, and Jed snags her by her waist and brings her to his side. "How's my baby?" He presses his lips to her stomach.

A pang of jealousy cuts me. I can't deny I want that too.

"How far along are you?" Ben asks. Thank goodness for him not staying on one topic very long.

Molly laughs. "Not too far along yet." She looks at the clock. "Speaking of... the oldest needs to be picked up from school and I'm thinking maybe her daddy should be the one to do it."

Jed stands and sighs. "Did you hear? Emelia is going apeshit about this baby. Thinks it's replacing her because it's a full part of us and she's only half of us." He shakes his head, and there's real concern in his eyes. It's rare to see Jed not carefree and fun loving.

"Maybe have Rylan talk to her," I suggest. "He's a Greene but not from either one of the original Greene families."

"If I can find that little fifteen-year-old, that's not a bad idea." Jed rubs his stubble with his palm.

"Hey," Xavier says. "Is he dating Calista Bailey now?"

Jed laughs and peers down at Molly, who snickers and says, "You know that was just a ploy to get you two together, right?"

"I knew that was the story, but I wasn't sure if that was actually the truth." Xavier shrugs.

"They still act like they don't like each other," Jed says.

"Kind of like you two," Molly says, waving her finger between Xavier and me.

Ben coughs, quickly grabbing his beer to wash down the food lodged in his throat. "Am I missing something?"

"Gotta go," Molly singsongs and walks away.

"People have been thinking we're secretly together for years. It's just a rumor. We're just friends. Right, X?"

He nods but doesn't say anything. Usually, he'd be the first one to point out that we're just friends.

Ben smiles. "Good. I was gonna ask if I'm just wasting my time here?"

"No." I give him a wan smile I hope appeases him. Although deep down I think the answer is yes, but not because of Xavier. Try as I might, my feelings for Ben just aren't moving in the direction of romance. Maybe I'm still too messed up about Xavier to allow someone else in.

"Then I can take you to dinner tonight? That Terra and Mare place."

I know Ben means well, but I don't want him to spend the night in a fancy restaurant he surely doesn't want to be in. "I have a better idea. How about we head to this bar on the outskirts of town? We can play pool and darts. I'll show you the spots off the beaten path of Sunrise Bay."

Ben's lips spread in a huge smile, revealing his perfect white teeth. "Sounds fun."

"Great. But now I have to get back to work. Um... my place?" I look at Xavier. "Would you mind showing Ben where I live? You have your key."

He doesn't make eye contact with me. "Sure."

"Okay, I get off at five, so I'll be home shortly after." I get up and put on my coat. "See you then." I open my purse to leave some money on the table.

"I got it," Xavier mumbles.

"I'll pay you back."

He nods.

This wasn't at all how I saw our lunch panning out, but I have no time to dwell on that. Fran and her crew made an appointment with me to discuss the extension and what they hope it will include, should they decide to donate money.

"Bye, guys." I walk off but turn around. "It's great that you came, Ben. Really."

I mean it. It was a nice thing for him to do, and if I was more into him, I'd be swooning right now. But his visit might be a blessing in disguise and let me really figure out whether there's anything between us.

His face brightens with a smile as though he never expected me to say that. "I'm glad I came then."

"Bye, X," I say and walk out the door.

Once I'm in the library and out of the public eye, I lock myself in my office for a moment to catch my breath and gain my equilibrium. Why do I feel as if I'm in some weird sort of love triangle when there's technically only one man who's interested in me?

Chapter Eleven

Xavier

"**D**oes this house suit her or what?" Ben asks the minute I use the key she hides in a rock garden by the front door to let us in. He should be staying at my place, but I wasn't gonna make some big deal about it and get Clara pissed at me again.

"It was her childhood home." I set the key on the table near the front door.

"Really? Where are her parents?" He leaves his suitcase in the front foyer and starts looking around. For some reason, it irks me that he'll be here alone. Then again, I've known Ben for many years—it's not like he's gonna steal her panties.

"She hasn't told you?" I stand inside the door, checking my watch because I don't want to be late picking up my dad from his treatment.

"No. This them?" He points at a picture in the living room from when she was little, her parents on either side of her.

"Yeah. They died." My chest tightens a little when I picture Clara's red eyes full of tears afterward.

His jaw hangs open when he turns toward me. "Seriously? Together?"

"No. Her dad died in a fishing accident, and her mom died of cancer a few years back."

"No siblings?"

"She has Presley, but she never even knew she existed until... wait? She hasn't told you any of this?"

Ben shrugs and ventures into the kitchen. "We haven't really gotten into the family thing."

I check my watch again and follow him. I only have a couple minutes. "What do you talk about?"

I love Clara's style because it's so uniquely her own, mixed with her mother's. The furniture is eclectic, different colors that go well together. There are always plants and flowers here, which I think she keeps on account of her mother's love for them. Although there aren't nearly as many as when her mom was alive. She's bought a few items for the house that make it appear more modern, but all in all, it's her. It's Clara.

"Whoa!" Ben says.

I turn the corner to find him out of the kitchen and in the living room, standing in front of her giant bookcase.

"Do you think she's read all these?"

"And then some. She's a librarian."

His finger scans one row. "She kind of intimidates me."

"How come?" I lean back against her small breakfast bar and cross my arms, watching him touch all her things and wanting to break his hands for it. I wish this feeling would disappear. Why the hell do I feel so territorial about him being in her space?

He turns to me, and I know what he's going to say from the insecure expression on his face. "She's smart. She reads. Sometimes I feel like our conversations aren't very smooth."

"You can read, right?" I joke, and he picks up a pillow off the couch and tosses it at me. I pick it up off the floor and wipe my hand down it, walking across the room to put it back. "Clara is..." I struggle with how to describe her because to me, she's just Clara, my best friend, my confidant, the first person I call when something good happens in my life. "She's just a woman like any other."

The lie tastes bitter. She's not like every other woman. She's down to earth and funny, and she cooks, but she's a better baker. She's sensitive and doesn't shy away from her feelings, and she lets others in even if they end up hurting her. She'll help anyone no matter the cost to herself.

"Even *I* know that's not true, X. She's not like any other woman I've ever dated." He picks up a book off the table and thumbs through it.

"True, but I can tell you there's no one with a kinder heart. You can trust her with your insecurities or anything else you're feeling in your relationship with her."

He laughs.

My brows furrow. "What?"

"It's funny you say that since you clearly never told her about your own hang-ups."

"Clara doesn't need to be bothered with my feelings of not trusting women."

He puts the book back down on the coffee table. "I'm gonna be honest here, X. I'm starting to feel like there's more to you two than friendship. Are you sure there aren't any feelings between you?"

I could be honest with him, let him know what went down two years ago, but I'm not going to betray Clara's trust like that. If she wants to tell him, she can.

"I'm sure."

He scrutinizes me for a moment as though I'm going to cave and change my answer.

"I gotta go get my dad. You okay here?"

His eyes scour the place. "What's there to do? It's only two o'clock."

I shrug. "You can go explore Sunrise Bay. If you head that way"—I point—"you'll go back by the bay."

"Okay. Sounds good. Hope Hank is doing well. Give him my best."

I nod and leave Clara's house, not liking leaving Ben in there alone.

On the way to the medical center, I turn on the radio to get my mind off Clara, but of course my stepsister Nikki's show—Scandals of Sunrise Bay—is on.

"I know I missed the morning shift, everyone, and I apologize, but my little man had a checkup with the doctor. I know you were in good hands with Chip anyway," she starts. "But I'm about to make it worth the wait."

"Do tell," Chip says.

"Well, I was on my way into the station when I heard a male voice calling for Clara. I stopped and turned to see Ben Noughton from the San Francisco Kingsmen running toward her like he was Superman. Literally. Instead of a cape though, it was his wheeled luggage flowing behind him. The man is massive."

"He's a wide reciever," Chip says as if that's explanation enough, which I suppose it is if you know football. "And isn't Ben your stepbrother's teammate?"

"Sure is!" Nikki's voice is way too upbeat for this to be a positive thing for me. "And Xavier was just opening the door to Truth or Dare Brewery for our little librarian, Clara Harrison."

Chip plays some sound they've been using lately during these stupid gossip sessions.

"Everyone knows Xavier is my stepbrother and I've known Clara for the same amount of time I've known him. I always thought there was something between them, then two years ago, their friendship crumbled out of nowhere. No one knew why. Well, I'm certain her sister, Presley, did, but she was so tight lipped you'd think her mouth was super-glued shut."

"They are family," Chip adds his two cents.

"Sure, but so am I. Anyway, back to today, because that's what matters. I got a phone call late last night about how Grandma Ethel and Dori had worked their magic, getting Xavier and Clara locked in Terra and Mare and forcing them to talk out their differences. Witnesses said they came out smiling, so I'm assuming all is right in the world with those two now. But then today when Ben Noughton announced his arrival into Sunrise Bay by calling Clara's name, Xavier looked anything but happy to see him."

"Are you suggesting that maybe Xavier and Clara aren't just best friends? That perhaps underlying feelings have started to surface?"

Damn Chip. I have no idea how an aging man handles gossiping with Nikki over the radio. I wish the two of them would mind their damn business and keep their opinions to themselves.

"I'm not sure. I have my feelers out, and I'm expecting a few people out there to report back to me if they spot anything to either confirm or deny that theory. But I don't think anyone in town would mind if those two finally admitted what we all already know—that they freaking want to see each other naked!"

I turn a corner and my hands grip the steering wheel a little tighter.

"It's been weird not to see Clara with his number on her cheek on game days the past couple years. Even this year, the first game of the season, she was doing inventory at The

Story Shop instead of being the biggest cheerleader for our hometown hero."

I hate the term hometown hero. They have no idea the pressure it puts on me to succeed. If I hadn't become one of the best quarterbacks in the league and had ended up back here, what would this town have thought of me then? That I was a failure, I'm sure.

"It's so romantic, right? Kindergarten friends to lovers, all they've shared together, the town librarian and the famous quarterback. The romantic comedy script practically writes itself." Nikki sighs dreamily.

"You have to be right first before someone can write it, and you know, some of his behavior in the past hasn't always put Xavier in the best light. That model he brought here when he was given that award at the high school, standing up on stage in the shortest dress ever during our late fall, was ridiculous. Everyone felt for Clara that day, sitting up in the stands when she should've been the one by his side, supporting him like she did for so many years."

"I'll give you that, Chip. Clara has always seemed like a woman who stands by her man. But I have to remind everyone on behalf of my stepbrother that they've never officially been an item. Sure, this town has shipped them together as a couple, but they weren't. Clara could've dated if she'd chosen to."

"Still, I always thought Xavier took Clara for granted."

What the fuck, Chip? Seriously?

"I don't know about that." At least my stepsister is sticking up for me. "He sure was there for her when her mom died. He couldn't stay here and play professional football. He had to leave."

Thank you very much, Nikki.

"I just didn't like the model thing. And showing up in a

limo... what the hell was that? He felt like a different guy back then."

I pull up to the medical office to get my dad and I'm torn between listening to the rest or turning it off and living happily in ignorance and bliss. Luckily, Nikki changes the topic to the new drink at The Grind and I'm thankful to not have my name on the radio any longer.

It's not that I'm not used to having my name in the press. I am a professional athlete. But it's usually to do with how I performed on the field, not my personal life.

Once I get out of my truck, I head into the medical office and up the elevator.

The receptionist smiles at me. "He's ready."

She buzzes me in, and I meet my dad where I do every time I'm able to pick him up—in the room where there's a recliner set up for him to receive treatment.

I love my dad. After my mom died, he turned into my everything. To watch him lose muscle mass because of being sick and not working all the time doing the physical labor his contracting job requires is hard to witness.

"What's up?" I say with a smile.

He gives me a sideways glance, and the nurse comes over to finish unhooking him from the IV. "I heard the radio. Nikki did quite the segment."

I can't help but roll my eyes. "Didn't she? I heard it on the way over."

"I hope you took my advice. If you're making Scandals of Sunrise, then I worry maybe you didn't hear me when you called me all those months ago." He moves to stand, and the nurse and I offer a hand, but he shoos us away to get up by himself.

I smile at the nurse as she says, "See you next time, Mr. Greene."

He grumbles something and I go to help him, but he walks ahead of me.

"Thank you," I say to the nurse.

"Oh, your dad is our favorite," she whispers. "Always so entertaining. Good luck." She looks at me as if she knows the whole sordid story of Clara and me.

"Yeah... okay."

I follow my dad down past the reception area, where he grabs a Dum Dum as if he's a little kid who just got a reward for getting his shots.

Holding up the Dum Dum after unwrapping it, he shakes his head. "I put poison in my body, and this is what I get? I'm a grown man. They can't spring for Blow Pops with the amount of money I'm paying them?"

I press the elevator button and it arrives in no time, then the two of us get in.

"I'll get you a bag of Blow Pops," I tell him.

"I don't want a bag of Blow Pops, it's the principle of the thing."

The elevator reaches the ground floor, and I lead my dad to my truck in the parking lot.

When I start the truck, my dad shifts to face me. "So, tell me, X, do you honestly love her as more than a friend?"

His eyes, so similar to my own, pierce into me. He might be the only one I can be honest with, but I'm not sure I'm ready to lay it all out there. I'm not sure I'm ready to admit to myself what I've felt brewing for a while.

When I don't answer, he says, "Take me to your mom's grave." When I stay still in my seat, he continues. "Son, put it in drive and take us to the cemetery."

"Okay," I say, my voice cracking.

Chapter Twelve

Xavier

 I stop the truck when we reach my mom's gravesite, except that instead of being here on our own, I'm four cars back because my siblings are standing up at my mom's grave.

"Did you ambush me?" I glare over at my father.

"You all share the same pain. Only the four of you can really understand what that's like and why it can be hard to move forward."

"I've moved forward. I'm not Cade."

My dad sighs. "I hate to break it to you, son, but you haven't." He opens the door and exits my truck.

I sit there a while longer, watching him walk to Mom's grave, each of my siblings glancing back at me when they hug him hello.

I grumble and turn off the ignition, open the door and follow him.

"Glad everyone could come," Chevelle says. "After Nikki's segment, it's definitely time we had this conversation."

"What?" I dare to ask when all eyes zero in on me. All three of my brothers have smirks I want to smack off their faces.

"You've completely lost your path and as your siblings,

we feel it's our responsibility to veer you back on course," Chevelle says.

"Like a lost cub who's strayed too far from his momma," Adam says. I give him a death glare and he holds up both hands. "Hey, I didn't call this family intervention."

"Let me guess... Chevelle? The girl who pretends she's not interested in anyone? The one who flirts with everyone but barely dates? Or was it Cade, who wants to tell me how great it is having a family once he got over his issues about loving someone as much as Mom? Or Fisher, who keeps everything he ever feels tucked up inside?" I'm not proud of my snide tone, but I'm not prepared for this confrontation.

"Well, it *was* me," Chevelle says. "I figure this is something Mom would do and without her here, I'm taking the reins."

I blow out a breath. I'd never give my baby sister shit for trying to fill in for my mom when I know how much guilt she holds inside because of how our mother died. "And what do you want from me?"

She shrugs. "We're all going to talk to Mom."

"But it's not her birthday." I push my hands into my jacket pockets.

"No one said we only have to do it on her birthday. Do you really only come here once a year?" she asks.

I shrug, because fuck yeah, I do. I'm reminded all the time that I don't have my mother on this planet anymore. Seeing her name inscribed in stone doesn't make it any more real for me.

"Let's move this along," my dad says.

"I brought little heart stones." Chevelle hands us each one to place on the headstone. "How about you start, Cade?"

He rolls his eyes, always acting like it's such a chore to be the firstborn.

"Hey, Mom, as you know, we had Leighton and she's perfect. Other than the fact that she doesn't sleep and Presley's one night away from going crazy. But you don't need to hear about the challenges, just know that Leighton reminds me of you. Even when she wakes up at two in the morning, she's laughing and smiling. Always so happy, just like I remember you. Except when I'd wrestle with these guys." He nods in the direction of me and my brothers. "Don't expect another one for a while though. One is more than enough for now." He positions the heart just so on her headstone.

Fisher takes a step toward the grave marker and starts speaking. "It's Fisher. You have no idea how much I'm holding in the urge to put Cade in a headlock right now. I'm not gonna do it though since we're here honoring you. I had twins for Christ's sake, can you believe that? So unlike Cade, neither of us gets to sleep through the night feedings." He eyes Cade and puts his heart on the stone. "Love you, always."

No one says anything for a few beats, we're all quiet, staring down at the stone.

"I'm pushing ahead," Adam says. "We've finally adopted Trey and I love him like my own, but our house isn't nearly as full as we want it to be. So send down an angel or two so Lucy and I can fill our house with love, will ya?" He sets the heart down next to Fisher's.

Chevelle stares at me and I roll my eyes. "Fine, I guess I'll go. Mom, I think it's safe to say that even though Cade can't suck up a few nights of no sleep and Fisher is still as pissy as ever, not to mention, Adam's quest to have a big family just like ours... there is only one of your children who need guidance right now." I blow out a breath, knowing I have to lay it all out there. I refuse to speak lies to my deceased mother. "One of us has lost our way, transformed into a man people loathed, hurt his nearest and dearest friend who he's developed feelings for, but can't bring himself to admit it." I set the small heart on the headstone and then groan. It was funny when Chevelle did this to Cade back when he was messed up about Presley, but not so much when it's me.

"We know he can change, Mom," Chevelle says, stepping forward and placing her heart down next to mine. "Thankfully he's broken up with Giulia, who definitely did not bring out the best in him. It's one step closer to being the Xavier we all knew and loved. Please help him get the rest of the way there."

I throw my hands in the air. "What do you all want me to do?"

"The question is what do you want to do? What are you scared of?" my dad asks and sits down on the nearby bench.

My shoulders slump. "I don't know."

"Listen, X," Cade approaches me. "If it's about you not wanting to get hurt by loving someone, I get it."

I shake my head. "It's not."

"Then why have you kept this distance between you and Clara? What happened two years ago?" Adam pushes.

"I don't want to hurt her... again." Silence fills the air.

"When did you hurt Clara?" Chevelle asks quietly. "Two years ago?"

I nod.

She reaches for my hand and squeezes. "How?"

I pull my hand back. "It doesn't matter. I just have to ignore this pull toward her and my feelings for her and eventually they'll go away. Some other guy will eventually come along and make her happy and he won't hurt her."

All my brothers chuckle under their breaths.

"Why are you all laughing?" I fight to keep my voice even.

"You think you'll be able to be her friend when she's married to some other guy?" Fisher asks.

"That you guys are gonna hang out all the time and she's gonna come down and see you play if there's another guy in the picture?" Adam says.

"Are you going to be her best man at the wedding and watch her marry someone else?" Cade asks.

I glance at my dad and he raises his eyebrows.

Fuck. Imagining that last scenario feels like imagining how I'll die.

"If you don't love her, we're not suggesting you go after her, but if you do... Xavier, you're wasting both of your time by trying to ignore your feelings," Chevelle says softly from next to me.

I shove my hands back into my pockets. "There's a lot you wouldn't understand. We live miles away from one another for one."

"Half the year," Cade interjects.

"All the gossip and shit? People will pick her apart on social media and I won't be able to handle that, neither will she," I add.

"Clara has an extensive vocabulary. She can hammer back if she wants to." Adam smiles at me.

"And—"

"Jesus Christ, X, do you want to be with her or not? Because I'm just coming off shift and Allie's gotta go to work. I was really hoping I'd catch her at nap time..."

Fisher doesn't have to finish; I get the point.

"All of you go," my dad says in a stern voice.

My brothers each clasp me on the shoulder and Chevelle hugs me. "Listen to your heart," she whispers. There's so much of our mom in her it seems crazy since she was only five when our mom died.

Once my siblings climb into their vehicles, my dad pats the empty side of the bench.

I walk over and sit next to him.

"I'll ask again… what are you afraid of?" he asks.

I shrug.

"Come on, it's me."

My dad made a point to have a relationship with each of us after our mom died. I think it's his way of filling both roles as mother and father because before my mom died, she did all the feelings stuff while he did the fun stuff.

I lean forward and sit with my forearms on my knees. "She's my entire life. Besides you guys, she knows me best."

"Maybe better?" He arches an eyebrow.

I nod, not wanting to admit there's plenty that Clara knows about me that my family doesn't.

"And you're willing to let it just slip away? How have the last two years been for you?"

Excruciating at first. I remember the loneliest of nights. Almost pressing the call button but stopping at the last minute. Typing out a text only to delete it. When something would happen in my life my first thought would be that I couldn't wait to tell Clara and then I'd remember that we weren't friends anymore.

"I had Giulia for part of it." It's a lame defense.

"Don't get me started on Giulia or your change of personality when you were with her."

"Yeah, I changed, and not for the better." I sit up and rest my back against the bench.

"Money and fame can do that to a person," he says. "Listen, Xavier, I understand being scared. Each one of your siblings were scared before they trusted their heart and happiness with another person. It's not an easy thing and I'm not here to suggest it is. Your mom died when you were eight and it sucks. But besides that, your life has gone pretty much how you've wanted, right?"

"Yeah."

"And you've been in control of it. If you bring in someone else, you lose that control. She could decide your way of living is too hard."

Exactly.

"She could leave you and break your heart."

I nod.

"She could get murdered by some stalker fan of yours."

I whip my head in his direction. "Jesus, Dad!"

"I'm kidding about that last one. But you know what else?"

"What?"

"She could love you until you take your last breath on this earth. She could not give one shit about what those petty trolls on social media say about her. She could win the hearts of your loyal fans. The two of you could spend the rest of your days happy—together."

When I don't say anything, he continues. "I know when something bad happens to you at a young age, it's hard to see the good over the bad. I don't tell many people this, but when I first started dating Marla, I would drive by her place to check up on her. Make sure she was alive and well because I was terrified of losing another woman I fell in love with."

"Huh," I say. "I didn't know that."

"At some point, I had to just enjoy the time I had with her. There are no guarantees in life, son. You're not born with a timer that tells you how many days, years, hours, or months you still have on this earth. You've had a great career but next year a life-threatening injury could cause you to retire early. So I think the only question you have to ask yourself is whether or not you love Clara. And if you do, then you need to find a way to stop holding yourself back and go after her with everything you've got." He pats my knee and stands. "I'll meet you at the truck."

I sit on the bench and read my mom's name, the years she lived and the titles she bore. Daughter, wife, mother. I've feared truly loving someone and giving them all of me for so long. Meanwhile, Clara was always there with her unconditional love and encouragement, always wanting what's best for me.

Of course, I love her.

Two years ago when those feelings of jealousy arose inside of me, I didn't know how to face them, didn't know what to do with them. All of a sudden Clara wasn't just my best friend, she was this alluring, sexy woman I wanted to have in my bed. I can't imagine a better life than one with her.

I shake my head and straighten out one of the hearts on top of my mom's headstone. "Wish me luck, Mom, I'm going to go fight for her."

As I walk back down the sidewalk to my truck, I swear I feel as if someone is hugging me.

Chapter Thirteen

Clara

I arrive home from the library to an empty house.

"Ben!" I call, but no one answers.

His suitcase is by the door, untouched. Maybe he's sleeping? I close the front door and walk quietly to the family room. The couch is empty. It doesn't look as though he's spent any time here this afternoon.

Upstairs looks the same. No sign of Ben.

I dig my phone out of my purse and call him. Fran and her posse were a lot to deal with today and all I want to do right now is sit on my couch, drink a glass of wine, and read an emotional book that will pull every frustrated tear out of me.

Nikki thought she was so funny with her little Scandals report today. Does she forget these are real people she's talking about? And Chip can bugger right off for acting as though I let Xavier walk all over me.

Fran was just the cherry on my shitty-ass day.

Ben doesn't answer his phone, but a woman does. "Hey, Clara, it's Molly. He's at Truth and Dare and um…"

I sigh, not wanting another issue to deal with today. "What?"

"Clary," Ben singsongs in the background. "Come drink with us."

"He might have had too much to drink. The grandma crew is here, and supposedly Midge challenged his manhood, and shots were consumed. Maybe too many shots."

My jaw drops open. "Why would you continue to serve him?"

"I didn't." She's quick to defend herself. "We're training a new person, so I don't have to help out anymore, but I had to run out because Emelia was throwing a fit. She didn't want Jed to take her to Brownies because it's a mother-daughter thing. I'm sorry. By the time we both got back here, the damage was done."

"I swear if those grandmas hired Emelia…"

"Doubtful. Although I'm not sure why Ben took the challenge on in the first place. But maybe you want to come down and get him."

I blow out a breath, ready to call Xavier because he's his teammate, but Ben came here to visit me. "I'll be right there."

After changing out of my slacks and blouse, I put on a pair of jeans, a bodysuit, and a sweater, then walk over to Truth and Dare since I live close to town.

The minute I walk inside the brewery, the grandmas all get up and collect their things.

"Nope. Sit." I point at their chairs.

Looking chastised, they do as I ask.

Ben looks at me and his smile is as sweet and innocent as a child whose mom is picking him up on the first day of kindergarten. As if he thought she wouldn't come back for him. And in this moment, I know I owe him the truth. It's glaringly obvious to me now that there can be no us.

The three grandmas try to talk first, but I put up my hand to silence them.

"Hi, Clary. These women thought they could drink me under the table, but I proved 'em wrong."

I look at the three very sober women and pick up a shot glass from in front of Ethel. I don't smell a drop of alcohol in the glass.

ETHEL SMILES TENTATIVELY. "My liver enzymes have been high lately."

"And the rest of you?"

Midge holds up her hands. "What can I say? He's a champ." She winks at Ben, and he makes this sound as if he's endeared by her.

"And Dori?"

She shrugs. "We couldn't let him woo you," she says, speaking the truth and raising her chin defiantly.

"You don't get to choose!" My voice is too loud, and I have to remind myself everyone in this town is already talking about me and this imaginary love triangle. I don't need to bring any more attention to myself.

"Bravo!" Molly claps from behind the bar.

All three grandmas give her a disapproving look, probably assuming they're responsible for her being with Jed.

"Come on, Ben. Let's go back to my place." I step forward to help him up.

"I got you flowers from the florist lady." He hands me a bouquet of mixed flowers off the table. "And a muffin from the coffee place." He hands me a bag with a mushed-up muffin inside. "Whoops, I dropped it, I think."

"That's okay. Come on."

"Here, let me help." Molly comes from around the bar.

"I already called my grandson. He can just put him in the bed of his truck," Midge says.

I whip my head in her direction. "He's not cattle, Midge."

"You two aren't going to be able to lift him," Dori says.

"You're going to strain something," Ethel adds.

"Exactly why you shouldn't have challenged him to a drinking game." I shake my head at them.

"We were just coming in for a drink," Dori says innocently. "Ethel was having a rough go with Hank being sick. We ran into Ben and started talking and he mentioned he'd come here to see you. Things kind of took on a life of their own. And so you know, he's figured it out."

I close my eyes for a beat. "I don't even want to know."

"He heard Nikki's segment on Scandals of Sunrise Bay like the rest of us. You and Xavier, it's written in the stars, dear," Ethel says.

"You can't deny it." Midge pushes up her dark glasses.

"We're just friends."

Ben leans his head on my shoulder. "You love him, don't you? I saw the box of pictures."

I suck in a breath. On the shelf of my bookcase is a box that has all the pictures of Xavier and me over the years. I took them down from all around my place after he brought Giulia to Sunrise Bay.

"Pictures, Ben?" Ethel perks up in her chair.

"None of your business." I give them my sternest look, which I don't think is very scary.

"I'm so stupid," he drawls drunkenly. "Of course he didn't want me to date you when I first asked."

"Ben, we're going to talk. Let's just get you to my house and sober you up, okay?"

"He's going to have to sleep it off," Molly tells me as if it's not obvious.

"I know, Molly!"

Ben stands and we each help lead him to the door.

Thank goodness he isn't so drunk that he can't walk, even if it isn't in a straight line.

"Hold up, we're coming to help," Mandi shouts from down the street, rushing over with that giant grandson of Midge's at her side. Interesting.

"Allow me," Noah says and slides Ben's arm over his shoulders to hold him up. "Hey, Ben, I'm a huge fan."

"Thanks, man. You from this town?"

"Nah, the one next door, Greywall."

"Sounds like a prison name," Ben says, and Noah laughs.

"Felt like that sometimes. Now let's get you home."

They both walk ahead without us.

"I gotta go back in. Good luck with breaking the big man's heart." Molly runs her hand down my arm.

"What's going on?" Mandi asks, eyes full of concern.

"I made a mistake. I never should've gotten involved with Ben. I tried, but... it wasn't a good decision."

"Because of Xavier?"

I roll my eyes. "If I hear that name one more time, I'm gonna scream."

We round the corner from the cobblestone streets in the downtown square to the back parking lot.

"X man!" Ben screams.

"Xavier Greene?" Noah says.

I look up and see Xavier getting out of his truck. Then I proceed to clench my fists and scream at the top of my lungs.

That didn't do much to solve my problem, since Butch from the Meat Market comes out his back door, as does Posey from Fringe, to see what's up. All eyes are on me, and I have no idea what to do, but red rage lights up inside me.

I glare at Xavier. "Why do you have to make everything so complicated?"

"Me?" He has the audacity to point at himself and look surprised.

"Yes, you. Now we're the talk of the town and one of your teammates is stuck in the middle of our shit."

"I just gave you the go-ahead to date him. What did I do?"

My breathing is heavy, and my chest is rising and falling as emotion overwhelms me. "You think you can tell me who I can and can't sleep with? Well, let me tell you something— I can sleep with whoever I want."

"Clara, let's just go home and talk about this, okay?" Xavier's hand touches my arm.

"No, I have to take care of Ben."

"I can take him to the inn. Keep an eye on him." Mandi's the fix-it girl of their family.

"No, this is my responsibility, but thank you for the offer."

"Put him in my truck," Xavier tells Noah, going over to help him.

"Just so you know, it was your grandma and her friends who got him drunk." I walk behind them to the truck.

"I'm not surprised." Xavier gets Ben in the back seat of his truck. "Come on, I'll drive you both back to your place."

I look back at Mandi and she looks just like I expected— as though she feels sorry for me. Another look I'm about done with in this town.

"Fine, then you can go home to your house." I climb into the front seat and belt myself in.

I overhear Xavier thanking Noah and Mandi. Mandi tells him if she needs anything to let her know, which he will not. Then he joins me in the front seat.

"Will you just talk to me?" Xavier says, looking at me from the corner of his eye while he pulls out of the space.

"I have nothing to say."

"I thought we were good. On our way back to being best friends. I'm sorry about Nikki, but you know I have no control over her."

I glance back at Ben. He's passed out. "It's not just that. In some twisted way, we've found ourselves hurting other people. Sooner or later, you need to figure out what you want."

"What does that mean?"

"I don't know. But we're not twelve anymore. Maybe the days of our friendship are over."

He reaches over the console of his truck for my hand, and I allow him the contact. Maybe because I'm scared of never feeling it again once I tell him everything I have pent up inside me. It's all come to a head. It's now or never, but first I have to get Ben taken care of.

"What does that mean?" he asks.

"We need to help Ben right now. It's both our faults he's in this position right now."

"I can't believe my grandma did this. Why would she?"

I huff because Xavier can't be this stupid, right? "You honestly don't know?"

He shrugs and makes a turn. "No. Other than she thought it would be a fun thing to brag about."

"She did it so I wouldn't go out with him. So I wouldn't sleep with him tonight. She did it as a way to make sure nothing happened that neither one of us could come back from. But what she doesn't know is that's already happened. It happened and I didn't speak up when I should have."

"Clara, I thought we put that all behind us?"

He pulls into my driveway, and I unlink my hand from his. "I thought I could, but it turns out I can't." I get out and open the back door. "Ben, come inside, let's get you to bed."

He kind of sits up and slumps over.

"I got him. Go unlock the door. I've taken care of him plenty in this state."

I do what Xavier says, and once we have Ben situated in the guest room and lying on his side, we both go downstairs to my kitchen.

My stomach feels light and tingly, my nerves getting the best of me. It's time for me to say to Xavier what I know I need to, what I know is best for me. But he won't want to hear it. Hell, I don't want to say it but I need to get the words out.

Chapter Fourteen

"I think we need to reevaluate this friendship."

Clara

I pull a bottle of vodka from my freezer and pour a good amount into a glass. But all it does is exactly what it's done every time I've pulled it out since that night two years ago... trigger memories of the night I spent in Xavier's bed.

We were out celebrating a win after a Thursday night game. I'd flown down to San Francisco because Xavier had asked me to be there. It was the anniversary of his mother's death, and since the day she died, I'd vowed to be with him every year after.

In years past, we'd spend the night watching a movie, making dinner, or hanging out with his family, but that year, we were at a bar with his teammates. One bar turned to two turned to hitting up some clubs. All the men had to do was walk up to the bouncer and we were let in. The star treatment wasn't something Xavier was always into, but I'd admit it was appealing to skip the line and have other women look at me as though I was the luckiest girl in the world.

At some point late in the evening, I took to the dance floor, dragging Xavier out by the tie he'd worn out of the stadium that night. Surprisingly it was still on, although it was loosened halfway down his chest.

Some of that night was a blur that's come back to me in snippets. At some point, Xavier left the dance floor and Ben was there.

I turned and it was his hands on my hips, my ass in front of his crotch. I finished dancing to the song because I didn't want to be rude to one of X's teammates. Plus, I knew Ben enough to know he was a flirt with everyone.

Afterward, I left the dance floor with the excuse that I needed a drink and found Xavier leaning against the wall, staring at me.

"Hey." I walked up and took a sip of his drink, which was surprisingly water. "Why did you leave me?"

"I had to take a piss," he said, anger laced through his tone. "So what, you just dance with anyone now?"

I looked over my shoulder and saw Ben had happily moved on to some redhead. "It's Ben." I handed his drink back to him. "What's with you?"

Someone bumped me and I was thrust into Xavier. His arm wrapped around my waist to steady me and our eyes locked. There was something so different in the way that he looked at me in that moment. He wasn't looking at me as if I was his best friend, but like I was a woman he desired.

"I don't like it," he said gruffly.

I laughed, but his fingers dug firmer into my hip. "What? Since when do you care who I dance with?"

"I guess since now."

The breath whooshed from my lungs. I shook my head as though he was joking. "What are you even—"

"Come on."

He took my hand and led us down the back hallway and out the rear door until we were back on the streets of the city. He flagged down a taxi. Since the club was about to let out, there was a line of them ready to take drunk patrons home.

"You just left your teammates," I said, not understanding this about-face.

"They're grown men. They'll manage."

He was silent the rest of the taxi ride, and the more I sat there and thought about it, the more anger boiled inside me. He had the audacity to get mad at me for dancing with one of his friends? Since when did he think he was my father?

The taxi pulled up to the curb and I didn't waste a second, letting myself out of the cab and stomping toward the building. His night doorman, Rowdy, hurried up out of his chair to open the front door for us.

"Hey, Rowdy." I bowed my head and stabbed the elevator button.

"Miss Harrison. Mr. Greene." He lowered his head in greeting.

"Thank you, Rowdy," Xavier told him as he came to stand next to me.

His arm touched my shoulder, and as though everything he was feeling siphoned through our point of contact, I felt the torrent of feelings inside him. I wondered if this was all because it was the anniversary of his mom's passing. She'd drowned in the lake by their childhood home when he was only eight. It had been early in our friendship, and he'd always kept those feelings close to his chest and I'd never pried. Maybe tonight was the night to do that.

The elevator arrived and we both stepped in. Xavier reached around me to press the button for his floor, and in doing so, his arm grazed my nipples. I inhaled a deep breath from the rush of heat that traveled between my thighs.

What was that?

When we reached his floor, I waited for him to open his door with his key, and when he did, he pushed the door open and motioned for me to enter first.

"Thanks," I mumbled.

I slipped off my heels as he stripped off his jacket and tie. I turned away and told myself to just go to bed and deal with this tomorrow when we were both sober, but I didn't. I swiveled around to find him toeing out of his dress shoes.

"I'm gonna be honest, I'm not sure where you get off being mad at me."

He concentrated on his shoes. "I didn't like it."

"Why? Because he's your teammate?"

He went to his freezer and pulled a glass from his cupboard, pouring himself a glass of vodka. "I didn't like seeing you with him."

I threw my arms in the air. "That sounds like a you problem."

He tipped back his glass and downed the vodka. "You're not getting it."

"Then explain it. Stop with this silent brooding you're doing because you're being an asshole. I didn't do anything wrong."

He rounded the breakfast bar, his eyes on me with such intensity I found myself stepping back. Not because I was afraid of Xavier, but because the air had shifted, and tension was building between us. Almost like the electric feeling in the air a millisecond before lightning strikes.

"I didn't like seeing you with him because it made me jealous as hell."

"What?" The word fell from my lips in a rush.

After all these years, would this be the moment? During a drunken night of celebration, me dancing with someone else is what pushes us out of the friendship zone and into the romance one?

"I just spent the entire taxi ride convincing myself not to do this."

My forehead scrunched up. "Do what?"

Before I could prepare, his hands clasped my cheeks, tilting my face up so he could dip down and kiss me. His lips were firm and not very welcoming at first. As if he wanted to make certain he felt nothing from our exchange. But then he tore his lips off me, and his hazel eyes ignited with something I'd never seen in them. I went to my tiptoes, and he pulled me into another kiss, but this time, his lips were soft, his tongue exploratory, begging for entrance. The minute I parted my lips, his hands left my cheeks and fell to the small of my back, pressing my body against his.

I'd fallen asleep on Xavier numerous times over the years, and I'd hugged him more times than I could count, but this was the first time I really felt the hardness of his chest with my breasts crushed against him.

Right as I was losing myself in him, he stripped his lips off mine. "I lost my mind seeing you out there with him."

My fingers weaved through his dark-blond hair, which he'd grown out a little this past season. "But what does all this mean?"

Even drunk, I couldn't stop thinking of the repercussions of what this meant for our friendship. I couldn't lose Xavier, and I was sure he felt the same way about me.

"For once, stop overthinking." He walked us backward to his bedroom while his hands fiddled with the zipper on the back of my dress.

When the backs of my legs hit the mattress, he smiled and his hands glided along my shoulders, slowly sliding my dress off my body. It fell to my feet in a pile and Xavier stepped back, taking me in.

I wanted to cover my half-naked body with my hands, because I knew the types of women Xavier had spent nights with. They were gorgeous, because of course they were. I was a librarian who loved nights with Ben & Jerry's or a bowl of popcorn with a good book. I lived in a state where you had no choice but to stay in the majority of the time because it was too cold and snowy. But if he didn't like what he saw, he never showed it.

"You're so beautiful, Clara. I knew you would be." He stepped closer and removed my bra, leaving me in only a sheer ivory thong.

His lips found mine, but the contact was brief as his lips

explored my body, casting small kisses down my chest and stomach until he was on his knees. His eyes and mouth were right in front of my center.

"X, we can't." I was practically panting. "Once we do this, there's no going back. I don't want to cross the line if it's not going to mean something, mean a change in our relationship."

"This is going to mean everything."

At his words the anxiety rinsed off my body like I stood in a rainstorm, sliding far away and out of sight.

He leaned forward and inhaled me, his knuckle running over my now-soaked panties, right between my folds. "Is this all for me?" His gaze never left from between my legs.

"Yes," I whispered.

He maneuvered his finger to the side of my panties and slid over the fabric. "Sit down and spread your legs."

I did as he asked, the mattress dipping under my weight. He gently dragged the scrap of fabric down my legs and tossed it behind him without a care. And with his hands on my knees, he spread me open with a groan from deep in his throat.

The sound made me want to keen. I was desperate for his touch.

I didn't have to wait long because he positioned his face between my thighs, swinging my legs over his shoulders and swiping me with his tongue. I wasn't sure where Xavier had learned how to do it, but he was masterful, as if he already knew my body, as if this wasn't the first time for us. His tongue dived, his mouth sucked, his finger delved. My back arched off the mattress, my fingers tightened in his blond strands, and my cries were loud and unapologetic.

My body was quick to reach the edge just based on the fact it was Xavier giving me this pleasure. Nothing about us in that moment felt awkward or weird because we'd been friends for so long. It just felt right, destined almost. Shivers came, then the tension that seized my body right before I climaxed snared me, and before I knew it, my orgasm was crashing over me. Sparks ignited my vision. Xavier slowed his movements, watching me come down from the high and the intensity of my orgasm.

"Fuck, Clara, you taste as sweet as you are." He climbed my body, pushing his finger into my mouth and allowing me to taste myself. He groaned when I sucked. "Are you on the pill? I'm clean."

I nodded eagerly. "Yes, and same."

I might've just finished, courtesy of Xavier's tongue, but I was desperate to have all of him. I needed to feel him inside me.

Without missing a beat, the tip of his cock pushed into my opening, and he sank into me as his hands swept the sweaty hair off my forehead. His gaze never strayed from mine, and it wasn't just sex in that moment. It was so much more.

His thrusts were slow, almost methodical, his eyes filled with so much more than lust. That was when it hit me—this was it. We'd crossed the line. He'd been jealous of me with another man. We were really going to do this.

His mouth fell to mine, and his hips circled at the same pace he kissed me. Somewhere in our slow, steady lovemaking, another orgasm crested inside me. Xavier's words tipped me over the edge.

"You feel so good."

"It's only ever been you, Clara."

"I would have never made it this far without you in my life."

"Fuck, woman. What are you doing to me?"

My fingernails dug into his strong shoulder blades, and I clenched the walls of my sex around his dick, earning a groan from him. I came only seconds before he stilled, emptying himself inside me.

We stared at one another afterward, and a flash of fear hit me that he might just pull away. But he smiled at me, kissed me again, and slid out of me, falling to his back.

It wasn't until the next morning that I realized my mistake—when alcohol is involved, it can take a while for someone to realize they think they made a mistake.

Xavier says my name and I blink to see him standing in front of me. We're no longer in that bed back in San Francisco, feeling like one. We're practically strangers, trying to find our way back to a friendship and standing in my living room in Alaska.

I sip my vodka, gaining the confidence to do what I need to survive. "I think we need to reevaluate this friendship."

Chapter Fifteen

Xavier

"Clara."

She blinks and looks at me. I smile, but she doesn't. She's mad. I can tell from her stiff shoulders and the glass of vodka in front of her, all telltale signs she's stewing over something.

I walk behind her, grab my own glass, and fill it with vodka.

She sips her drink. "I think we need to reevaluate this friendship."

I almost spit out my vodka, but I struggle to swallow it and stare at her in disbelief. "What?"

"We're hurting people. We hurt Ben." She points upstairs. "All because you can't figure out what you want."

"You're putting this on me?" I point at myself. "You were pissed at me because you wanted to date him, and I said no. Now I didn't stand in the way, and you decide I'm somehow to blame?"

She rubs her forehead then strips off her sweater, leaving her in a tight bodysuit that only shows off the curve of her tits. How many times have I seen her in less and never thought about touching them the way I am now? What the fuck is wrong with me?

"I wanted to like him. I did. I didn't want you to tell me what I could do and couldn't do."

"Then it's just a failed dating experience between the two of you. I'm not sure how I come into it."

She stares at me for so long I swallow the dry lump in my throat.

"Let me ask you a question. What do you want from this?" She waves her finger between us. I down the rest of my vodka and reach for the bottle, but she snags it first. "We're doing this sober this time around."

Can I confess to her the torrent of emotions coursing through me? I'm not even sure I understand what they all mean. "I don't know. I'm confused."

She nods and points at me. "And that's why we need to part ways." She takes the bottle and heads toward the couch.

"Clara, that's not a solution."

"It is. I can't even look at you. I feel like you're playing games with me, Xavier. Not on purpose. I don't even think you know you're doing it. But I see the way you feel when Ben's around and I know what it meant the first time you acted that way." She lets a long sigh leave her lips. "Do you know how hard it is to not have you in my life? I ached for our friendship every day." She turns to look at me and there are tears in her eyes.

It's like a stab to the chest. "You think I didn't feel the same?"

"I don't know what you feel. I don't think you do either. But do you know how embarrassing it is to live in this town and hear what people say about us?"

"We've always said screw them." Ever since we were young, we've heard the jokes, the whispers that we were more than friends.

"Everyone thinks we belong together, and I have to listen

to it constantly when I know the reason why we're not. That one night we crossed the line and the next morning you woke up with regrets. And then you brought your new persona and your new girlfriend back here—which I realize you're entitled to do, but that hurt me… so much."

I could crumble to the ground right now. I've never felt like a bigger piece of shit. I didn't bring Giulia to Sunrise Bay to hurt Clara. She was so pissed at me that I didn't think she'd even care.

Shame has me staring at the floor. "I lost myself for a little bit there. Allowed that five-year deal to get in my head."

She nods, and a tear slips down her cheek when I look back up at her. "Justified or not, I was humiliated when you stood on that stage with your arm wrapped around her waist. I was the one back here, having to answer all the questions everyone had after you left, dealing with every-one's 'poor Clara' looks whenever I'd run into someone." Her head falls forward in what looks like defeat. "So." She picks up her head and wipes her tears. "You need to leave."

Standing and turning on her heel, she heads toward the front door, and I hear it open.

I walk into the foyer, more determined than ever to make her understand how sorry I am for hurting her. "I'm not leaving."

"The choice isn't yours. You can be Mr. Hotshot back in San Francisco, but here, you're just Xavier Greene, townie." She taps her foot on the hardwood floor.

"We're finishing this once and for all. I'm not gonna let us throw away all these years of friendship because I stuck my dick in you one night."

She gasps and winces, and I regret my words. God, I'm such an asshole. Why am I fucking this up so much?

"Jesus, you know what I mean." I clench my hand in my hair.

She doesn't look up from the floor. "Yeah, you've already made it clear that it was just sex to you."

I want to fall on my knees and tell her it wasn't, but a hurricane of emotions are assaulting me, and it feels as though the hurricane is barreling down on me and I'm trying to hammer the wood boards over the windows in order to protect myself.

Fuck, before I can think about what might come as a result of me being totally honest, I let the words leave my lips. "It wasn't just sex, but I don't know what to do with that."

She looks at me, disappointment and sadness like a coat of paint over her beautiful features. "I don't have the fight inside me anymore, X. Do what you want. I'm going to bed."

She releases the door, and it slowly closes until I hear it click shut. She walks past me, her shoulder brushing my arm, and I grip her hand before she gets too far. She stays where she is, facing away from me, and I stare at her back.

"I can't lose you," I say softly.

"At some point, I have to move on. I can't keep waiting for you."

I gently pull her back and turn her to face me. "I know. That's why I stepped aside for Ben. Don't mistake my will-ingness to do it for your benefit for me not caring. It just about killed me to do it, but I knew if I didn't, there was no way we could be friends again."

"I wanted it to work with Ben. I wanted these feelings for you to go away. I wanted to get back to when I only saw you as my best friend, but I'm not sure I can anymore. I don't think I knew that until we made up."

"Yeah, I'm not sure I can either." I place a hand on her

cheek, and she nuzzles into my hold, our gazes locking. "I love you, Clara. So fucking much."

That much I know is true. Regardless of what I can or can't give her, I can admit that I love this woman with my whole heart.

She squirms out of my hold. "I know."

"But what?"

Clara wraps her arms around herself and bites her lower lip. "You can't keep messing with my life."

"What do you want from me?"

"I only ever wanted honesty."

I step toward her, putting my hands on her upper arms. "You know my demons."

She shakes her head. "Everyone has them, X."

"Mine cripple me."

"I know." She frowns and her eyes water.

Damn it. I wish I could snap my fingers and give her exactly what she wants. "My life isn't made to have a partner I love be a part of it. You think Scandals of Sunrise Bay is bad? Try the tabloids. Try having other women hate you just because you're with me. Shaming you for every little thing you say or do or wear. God, I wouldn't be able to handle seeing you go through that. Plus, the distance alone. There's a reason people say no to long-distance relationships. They don't fucking work. How the hell will I concentrate on my job when all I'll be thinking about is how far apart we are? I'd always be counting the minutes until the next time I could get my hands on you. Wondering what you're doing. Missing you and wishing I was with you. If you were my everything, how the hell could I ever stand to be apart from you?"

Instead of the understanding I was hoping to find on her face, I see only irritation.

"That's fine. But I'm not gonna stick around until your glory days are over. Until you fuck your way through Gucci's model lineup and enjoy your party days, then when your career is finally over, you come back to poor ol' Clara, your BFF town librarian."

I step toward her. "Is that what you think? That you're somehow second best?"

She says nothing.

"Tell me."

She looks me square in the eye as if to challenge me, but I know she's about to slice me open. "I didn't. Not until the morning after you made love to me and pretended that you didn't feel a damn thing."

It's like my guts spill out onto the floor, I feel that hollow.

She walks away from me into the kitchen.

I rush to catch up to her, grab her elbow, and twist her around, then mold my hands to her hips. "Let me clear up a few things for you. That night, I was jealous and drunk, but I never regretted one moment of our time together. Not one second. In fact, it's been on repeat in my head for two fucking years. I started dating Giulia to get you out of my head, but all I ever did was compare the two of you and she never measured up. I've tried to protect you my entire life."

"I don't need your protection. I manage just fine on my own."

"Just listen to me, will you?" I snap.

"What?"

God, she's so stubborn and frustrating. I do the only thing I can think of to get her to understand—I smash my lips to hers. At first Clara's stiff as a board, but she slowly sinks into my hold, opening her mouth for me.

God, she feels so good in my arms. So right.

One heavy push from her to my chest and we're back to

being feet apart. Clara wipes her mouth with the back of her hand. "You can't do that."

"It's me telling you that I do want you in my life and I want you as more than a friend. I'm not sure what that looks like at this moment, but it's always been you, Clara. Always."

She stares at me so long that I shift my stance. "Xavier, you need to figure that out before anything happens between us again. I can't just be your friend anymore. It's too painful."

She's right. It's about time I figure out my shit because I've hurt Clara enough and she's the one person I never want to be in pain.

"You can have the couch. I'm going to bed." Without another word, she turns and walks out of the room.

Why does my chest hurt as though she's walking out of my life again?

AT THREE IN THE MORNING, a loud banging in the kitchen wakes me. I peer over the couch to see Ben rummaging through the fridge.

"Hey," I say, and he startles.

"Damn, man, you scared me." He rests his hand on his head. "What happened last night?"

I get up from the couch and head over to the stools by the breakfast counter. It's time to come clean with my friend. "I need to apologize."

"Why?" He pours a glass of water and downs it, then refills it.

"I should've never said it wouldn't bother me if you got Clara's phone number. It did. Way more than I let on and I should've been honest with you from the start."

He sits next to me with a frown. "How so?"

"Two years ago, we slept together." Hopefully Clara's not pissed I've told him, but knowing her, after our conversation last night, she was planning to do the same anyway.

He shrugs with a resigned expression. "I'm not that surprised. I don't really believe in the opposite sex being strictly platonic friends. Besides, I could tell she wasn't that into me. Hell, my trip up here was a Hail Mary. I'm ready to be more serious with someone and Clara's not like most of the women we meet in our line of work."

I chuckle. "Truth. You're not pissed?"

He clamps me on the shoulder. "Nah, man. It is what it is. So, if you guys slept together two years ago, how come you're not an item? What happened?"

I chuckle because that's Ben for you. Always easygoing and affable. "I was an idiot and told her the next morning that I didn't feel the same as she did. That I only wanted to be friends."

"And that's how you felt?"

"Only because I was scared."

"Scared of what?" He sips his water.

I shrug. "It's complicated. My mom died when I was eight—in front of me—so I'm not really keen on the whole loving someone to lose them thing." I suppress a shudder when I think of the look on my dad's face when he was trying to revive my mother. It's seared into my brain, and I know I'll never forget it. "Add on the fact that our career choice doesn't exactly make a relationship easy."

"Sure, but plenty of people have them. Ashton is going strong now."

I nod. "You know all the shit the girls get from other women on social media."

He looks upstairs to where Clara is probably sleeping.

"You know I lost my mom when I was young too. Hell, it's why I'm so inept with talking to women probably—I had zero female influence growing up. But that woman up there can handle herself. And guess what? Maybe you're worth it to her. But you have to let her decide whether she thinks you're worth the risk, not decide for her. If you put away all your doubts, I think you'll realize you're missing out on a pretty great life you could be having with her at your side."

"Yeah, but—"

"Jesus, X, stop with the buts. What would've happened if when the scouts called, you said, 'Well, I don't know... some players get hurt, some players don't pan out.' Or after you got drafted if you said, 'But what if I never win a ring or what if the media chews me apart?' Be the same man who made his dream come true and go be the man of her dreams." He smiles and winks. "Oh, I like that line."

Who would have guessed that Ben would be the one to get through to me? Before I can say anything, he continues.

"My mom dying taught me one thing. Life is short. You never know when your time is up, so why wouldn't you want to spend every minute being with the person you love? Don't listen to those inner demons. You live your life scared, you'll die with regrets."

My eyebrows rise. "Man, you're just coming out with all the inspiration lines."

"I was reading one of Clara's books before I got bored and explored downtown, which, did you know your grandma and her friends challenged me to a drinking contest? And I did it?"

"Afraid so."

He shakes his head. "I'm going to try to sleep for another couple hours. I'll see you later." He claps me on the shoulder again.

"Ben? I'm sorry you got caught up in all this."

"It's cool, man. If me going after the girl you want gets you to finally make a move, it's all worth it in my eyes. Plus, we both know her heart was already taken. Don't worry about me. One day I'll find my own Clara." He winks and heads up the stairs.

I chuckle, and I hear him do the same as he makes his way up the stairs. I sit at the counter for another hour, figuring out where I go from here and how I'll ever convince Clara that she can trust me with her heart.

Chapter Sixteen

Clara

I wake up late the next morning and pull a sweatshirt on over my cami, leaving me looking a little like a hot mess in my sweatshirt and flannel pants, hair in a high ponytail. But it's probably better anyway, given the conversation I need to have with Ben.

The house is quiet, and the guest room door is open. I spot a note on the pillow of the made bed. I pick it up and read.

Thank you for letting me crash here, and I apologize for anything I might have said last night in my drunken state. You don't have to worry about sparing my feelings. I'm a big boy and I talked to Xavier. I would never want to step in the middle of true love. I have a request, and by all means you don't have to do it, but I think in the long run it will do you good... give the guy a chance. Sometimes big-ass grown men who play professional football still get scared. ;) Catch you next time you're in San Fran.

~ Ben

I SMILE at the note and feel a little pang of sadness. Ben is a good man, and I hope he finds his person someday soon. I take the note downstairs, expecting to see Xavier on the couch, but that too is empty. The blanket and pillow have been put back in the closet I keep them in.

As though the two men are somehow the same person, there's a book on the coffee table that I know wasn't there before, a piece of paper sticking out of it. I sit on the couch and open the book, taking out the letter written on the back of a bill that sat on my counter.

CLARA,

I'VE BEEN A FOOL, and I don't expect you to trust in everything I told you last night. Not yet anyway. I've been so hung up on my fears that I forgot how I got to where I am in my life right now— by conquering my fears, pushing them out of the way, and moving full steam ahead.

Until two years ago, I hadn't felt as terrified as I did when I saw my dad pull my mom from that frozen lake. But when I woke up after our night together, I felt practically paralyzed by fear because it felt to me, at the time, like I had risked the most important person in the world for one night together. That feeling caused my life to spin out of control, and as hard as I tried to grasp for some sort of normalcy, it never came. The more scared I got, the more I changed and the more I leaned into the new image of who I was.

It was so wrong of me to ever bring Giulia to Sunrise Bay or really date her at all, knowing I'd already fallen for you. I'm sorry. From the bottom of my heart, I apologize.

I'm writing this letter early in the morning rather than telling you this to your face because I don't want to chicken out like I have so many times before.

I don't expect you to just forgive me. Nor do I think you would. I want to prove it to you. Prove to you that I'm the man you're supposed to spend the rest of your life with. It'll be tricky with me thousands of miles away from you, but I will persevere. And when my season is over, I will be running back to Sunrise Bay for you.

Keep an eye out for my wooing.

Love you always,

X

THIS ISN'T AT ALL what I thought I'd be waking up to this morning. I assumed Xavier would take back everything he'd said in the heat of the moment last night. I knew we were at a crossroads, but for him to say he's going to openly pursue me is unexpected and surprising and, if I'm honest with myself, a little thrilling.

In an effort to clear my head I set out to get my running gear together, but the doorbell rings. I open the door to find Amy from Twisted Stem with a vase full of red roses and an envelope where the card would be.

"I told him I'd deliver these personally. And don't worry, I'm not telling a soul who sent them to you." She winks and hands them over.

I smell the roses, and it might be cliché, but it's so classically romantic. Red roses have one meaning and that's love.

After thanking Amy, I set the vase on the counter, pull out the envelope, and open it to find a check with way too many zeros, made out to the Sunrise Bay Library. The small note just says, "Build your extension. You of all people deserve it."

The fact that I hold all the money I need to build the extension is electrifying even though I know there's no way I'm going to keep it. Quickly, before I can change my mind, I rip it into small pieces. I hope this isn't how he thinks he's going to win me over—with money.

Picking up my phone, I send a text to Xavier.

> FYI I'm not for sale.

The three dots appear immediately, as if he watched Amy deliver the flowers and was waiting for my response.

> I'm doing it for the town. I won't even ask you to name the extension after me.

> This is you buying me off. Try something else. And void the check, I tore it up.

> CLARA! Why? This way you can break ground in the spring.

> You know I don't work that way. I do love the flowers though. Thank you :)

> Can I call you tonight?

I take a moment to think about it, but as scared as I am to put myself out there for Xavier to hurt me again, I still trust him. There's too much past, too much between us for me not to give us another chance at romance.

> Yeah.

> Eight?

> Okay.

I toss my phone on the counter. I definitely need to clear my mind now.

On my run, whether I do it subconsciously or not, I end up at the high school stadium. The metal gate leading to the track is open and I decide to walk around it to cool down.

My mind wanders and before I know it, I'm remembering the night I'd planned on talking to Xavier in the hopes of patching up the hole in our friendship.

I pulled into the parking lot of the high school, which was already packed with cars since it was Xavier's big night. I'd prepared myself for his entire family to be there and Presley assured me she'd be by my side the whole time.

Xavier was being honored before the high school football game and I figured he'd do a quick in and out of town, but surely, he'd make time for dinner with his family or something after the ceremony the way he always did. I'd planned to catch him on the way in or out that night.

My first clue that things were not going to go how I'd hoped was when I spotted the limo that sat idle along the curb. There was no way anyone else in Sunrise Bay would've had a limo bring them to a high school football game, but even that was outside of Xavier's character. He never showed off his wealth or his fame to the people in town. In fact, he did everything he could not to make anyone in his hometown feel less than. In Sunrise Bay he was Xavier Greene, son of Hank Greene and Laurie Greene, grandson to Ethel Greene and just a good hometown boy.

As I got out of my car, I looked over at the limo to see Cameron Baker, Fisher Greene and his baby mama, Allie standing beside the long black vehicle.

My gaze traveled to who they were standing with. They weren't hard to miss. The model, Giulia, who Xavier had been photographed with a few times stood at his side in the skimpiest dress. She had to be freezing. Xavier wore a three-piece designer suit that made him appear better than everyone in their jeans, sweaters, and winter jackets. Even the way he held himself was different. His chin was tipped up, his chest pushed out a little more and he had this look on his face like he was only half-interested in what was going on here tonight, even though he was the guest of honor.

All I remember thinking was how beautiful they looked together.

"Clara!" Cam raised his hand at me as if I didn't see him.

My name caught Xavier's attention and he turned away from whoever he was talking to. Our eyes locked and a million words floated on the breeze across the asphalt. It didn't take long though before Giulia slid her arm through his and pulled him back into the conversation they were having.

My stomach twisted painfully. It was clear the night wouldn't go as planned, so I ambled over to the group, trying to preserve some of my dignity by not just fleeing in the other direction like I so badly wanted to do. I tried to put on a bright face and distract any attention away from myself by putting it on Allie and asking if I could touch her belly.

I could feel the eyes of everyone in town on me, looking for my reaction. They didn't know what had transpired between Xavier and me—they only knew that we were no longer best friends. The rumor mill would be working overtime tonight with theories about how I felt that Xavier had brought Giulia, what it meant that we hadn't spoken, and wondering about how Xavier had seemed to change.

Chevelle arrived moments later and after we found Presley on the bleachers and sat next to her. I swallowed the bile rushing up my throat when Xavier was called up and Giulia was at his side and pretended not to be bothered by the way everyone who looked at me gave me a smile that indicated that they felt sorry for me.

"Did you see Xavier?" Fisher asked Cade.

He rolled his eyes. "Think fame has gone to his head?"

"He looks like a GQ model instead of a pro quarterback," Jed chimed in.

"Okay, guys, let's give him a break," Hank said.

At least I wasn't the only one who sensed the change in Xavier.

"How isn't she blue when she's only wearing an inch of fabric?" Posey asked, unimpressed.

"Fashion over common sense, I suppose," Presley said. Her hand slid out from under her blanket and squeezed my knee before she leaned in close. "Are you still going to talk to him?"

I watched him walk up to receive his award with an unfamiliar arrogance on his face, Giulia on his arm. The longer they stood there the more eyes I felt on me. Sure he had every right to bring the woman he's seeing with him tonight, but right or wrong it still felt like a slap in the face after all that had transpired between us. Everyone in town thought that Xavier and I had crossed the line and now I'd been cast as the scorned best friend and lover.

Xavier walked off the stage, careful to hold Giulia's hand so her heels didn't get stuck and off the field without a backward glance. I knew in that instant that our friendship was over.

AT EIGHT O'CLOCK, my phone rings and Xavier's name shows up on my screen. A strong set of butterfly wings flap in my stomach. Actually, they feel more like bird wings. I place my hand over my stomach to calm it. I do not need to get my hopes up right now.

"Hello?" I answer.

"Hey." His voice is the same one I've been used to my

whole life. Casual and suave, like he's just lying on the couch. "How was your day?"

"Good. I went for a run and spent probably one of the last days sitting by the bay before it gets too cold."

I'd gone there to think. To be alone.

"And?"

Unfortunately, Xavier knows my rituals. He knows that when things are chaotic in my life, I go to the bay and watch the water while I sort things out in my mind. "You assume I was thinking about you?"

"Were you not?"

"No, I was."

"And?" he asks.

I pick at some imaginary lint on my leggings. "I want to give this a try, but I'm scared. Especially after what happened the last time we changed things up."

"I know. I'm scared too, but everything worthwhile is scary, right?"

I laugh and lean back in the chair. "What made you do a one-eighty so fast?"

"Ben reminded me that I was scared shitless starting everything I've ever gotten in this life—our high school state championship, my D1 scholarship, the draft, my first Super Bowl. The first day of kindergarten—until a little girl with brown pigtails befriended me."

I scoff. "Oh please. You know as well as I do that you'd have made friends with the boys. Which you did."

It's silent for a while.

"What were you thinking about at the bay? Specifically."

Two years ago, I wouldn't have thought twice about sharing such vulnerable things with him. But since the number one thing I realized was that I need him to be vulnerable with me, I have to be open and hide nothing from him if this is ever going to work.

"You barely talk to me about intimate topics. Like what you're scared of, for instance."

"You knew I was scared before the draft. Remember when I snuck outside right before they called my name? You were the one who told me it was okay to be scared and it didn't matter if I was drafted first or thirty-second, it was what I did once I landed on a team that mattered."

I inhale over the fact that he remembers that. "What about your fear of relationships? Unresolved fears from your mom dying…"

A long stream of air flows through the receiver. "I've just always kept those things to myself."

"Well, you don't have to. Whenever you're ready, I'm here."

"I'll tell you one. I fear I've failed you in our friendship. You've always been there for me, and I've never been there for you. Is our friendship one sided?"

I laugh. "You listening to Chip?"

"On the plane ride, I thought about it, and I think he might have a point."

I shake my head even though he can't see me. "He doesn't. You were there for me when my mom died. Unlike you, I've always been an open book and you've never made me feel anything but understood. You listen to me whether it's about Fran and her crew on my back for something at the library or I'm complaining about tourist traffic. So, I've never felt that way, Xavier. Ever."

He doesn't say anything.

"I would tell you… I'm not a doormat, X."

"Okay," he says, but he sounds as though he's not completely sure he believes it.

"Tell me about the season."

Since I don't think he's going to open up to me right now, I figure let's start out easy.

"I'd rather hear about the expansion."

I shake my head. "Well..."

We talk for another hour, and I reluctantly hang up, knowing he has practice in the morning.

I get ready for bed, and as I slip under the covers, I struggle to fall asleep, my mind unable to stop swirling. I smile, remembering some of the things he said and the sound of his voice.

As my eyes close, I'm certain I won't be able to go in halfway because Xavier's always been my number one person. Might as well jump off the bridge with both feet and have faith that he's right next to me, as scary as it is.

Chapter Seventeen

Xavier

Thanksgiving at the Greene's is as chaotic as people probably imagine. There've been years that I was grateful to have to play on Thanksgiving, as sad as that is. But this year, it felt as if the flight to Alaska took forever.

Clara and I have been talking over the phone for the past month, and it feels as if we're back to normal. At least the friendship part. I'm not sure about our romantic relationship, since it's hard to tell when you're miles apart from one another. And it's not like I'm going to try to woo her by suggesting phone sex.

I ring her doorbell, and just the sounds coming from the inside of the house that tell me she's on her way to open the door make me edgy. Knowing she's in there and I'm moments from seeing her beautiful face makes me anxious. Usually I'd have walked right in, used the key she never asked me to give back. The key I put in a drawer in my house when we weren't talking. I still haven't put it back on my key chain. I'd rather wait until it feels right.

The door opens and I shove my hands in my pockets, so I don't rush forward and pull her into my arms and kiss her until we're both breathless. I've missed seeing her face. FaceTime doesn't cut it.

"Happy Thanksgiving." She beams and steps aside to let me in.

"Happy Thanksgiving." I kiss her cheek. Sooner or later, we have to grow comfortable with physical affection, but I'm not sure what she's comfortable with yet, so I'm playing it safe.

"Come in. I have to get my side dish packed to go over. How was your flight?"

I follow her in, my eyes on her ass in a tight pair of jeans. "Too long."

"Yeah, but you've got two days off." She pulls a casserole of cheesy potatoes out of the oven where she was keeping it warm. It's her specialty dish, the one she's always responsible for at my family's house.

I help her put it in the carrying case. "This is the first year, other than my rookie year, that I wish the season was over already."

She bites her lip. "Why would that be?" The flirtatious glint in her eye says she knows exactly why.

"There's this hot blonde I've been talking to. She lives in this small town far away and I can't stop thinking of her."

A blush rushes to her cheeks, and she shakes her head. "X."

"I'm serious. It's so hard to concentrate on the game when I only want to see you. I feel like we're stalled until I come home for good."

She zips up the carrying case and faces me. "We're not. The phone conversations are doing us good. And your abundance of gifts tells me everything I need to know." She looks over to her fireplace mantel, where all my flowers sit. "Which you don't have to do anymore."

"Yes, I do." I step closer to her, and she inhales. Her back is against the counter, and I place my hand on her cheek, running my thumb over the apple of her cheek where her blush grows pinker. "Can I kiss you?"

Her eyes give me the answer I want, but I wait for the words. "You don't have to ask."

I lean forward and press my lips to hers. She moans and I press my lips firmer, my tongue seeking entrance. She willingly parts her lips and our tongues dance in a rhythm we haven't yet perfected, but having her like this in my arms, with our lips locked... I never want to be away from her. I slowly close the kiss but don't step back.

Her hands are spread on my chest. "We should go."

"We should stay here and say screw my family."

She tilts her head, giving me the expression that says that can't happen. "Speaking of."

"What?"

"Are we friends today?"

I hear the hitch in her voice. The unsteadiness that says she thinks I'll say yes, and this past month meant nothing.

"I was going to talk to you about that." I take her hands. "What are you comfortable with? Have you told anyone?"

"Just Presley," she says, which I expected.

"I'll leave it up to you. I'd like to be honest with them."

She nods. "Okay, if you're sure."

"Clara." I place my finger under her chin and urge her to look me in the eye. "I'm positive. I'm in this. One hundred percent."

She nods enthusiastically as though she wasn't doubting me, but it's clear a mantel full of red roses won't heal the wound I caused. "I know."

"Do you?"

"I do. I'm just protecting myself still, I think, and I second-guess things."

"Once I get back here after the season, I'll prove it to

you." I kiss her one more time. This one is short and brief. "Come on. We're about to make Marla's day."

She laughs and I pick up the carrying case, leading us out the front door.

AFTER I PULL out of her driveway, I reach over the console and take Clara's hand. It's soft, and as our fingers link, I can't stop myself from looking at her when we hit a stop sign. She smiles my way, and all feels right in my world.

It was clear when I was jealous that I had feelings beyond friendship for her, but for some reason, after giving myself permission to explore a romantic relationship with her, in just a month it's like I'm some lovesick teenager.

"I'm gonna be honest, I'm a tad apprehensive telling your family," she says.

"Why?" I squeeze her hand.

She glances my way. "What do you think they'll think of us?"

"They're going to be thrilled. They seemed to know what I didn't realize for years."

She swivels in her seat to face me fully. "I do want to clear that up. I mean, I wasn't pining over you for years."

I park in the driveway of my dad and Marla's place. Laughing, I turn off the ignition. "I didn't think that."

"Are you sure? I mean, I started thinking maybe there could be more between us, like, a year at most before we slept together. But mostly, the night that we did, it just felt so right that I grasped onto the idea of us. And then after I knew what it was like for the two of us to be together, I was really invested. But I don't want you thinking I was some lovesick puppy for years."

I tighten my grip on her hand. "Are you trying to tame my ego, or just want to make sure I don't take you for granted?"

She sighs, her eyes darting behind us to another vehicle pulling up.

"Clara?"

"I just don't want you to think I was looking at you differently all those years we were friends."

"Noted." I nod.

"I mean—"

I cut her off with a kiss. She lets out a little sound of surprise but sinks into the kiss, her hand wrapping around the back of my head, her nails running through my short hair.

TAP. TAP.

Clara backs up and wipes her mouth as if there's evidence of us.

I turn to see Cam standing by my window with his jaw hanging open.

"Now or never. Let's do this," I tell her.

I climb out of my truck and Cam pats me on the back. "Finally. You might be the dumbest fuck I know."

I don't say anything about the fact that he stares at my baby sister as if she's his favorite dessert.

"Don't go blabbing it, okay?" I grab the carrying case with Clara's dish from my back seat, and all three of us walk up the driveway together.

"I can keep secrets, unlike most of you Greenes." He tips his head toward Clara. "Looking good."

I put my arm around her, and she giggles.

"Getting all protective already, huh?" Cam laughs and walks in through the garage first.

I give Clara one more look to say we've got this, and we follow him into the house.

The minute we walk in, it's as if we entered a day care. There are babies crying everywhere, and as I walk into the family room, Emelia runs past me in tears, then up the stairs.

"Damn it!" Jed yells and goes to follow her.

"Give me a minute," I say to Clara, who nods and takes the dish from my hands.

I follow Jed up the stairs. I completely forgot that when I was in town before, I'd wanted to talk to Emelia.

Jed's knocking on Posey's old bedroom door when I approach. He shakes his head. "My little girl went from a sweetie pie to *Firestarter*."

"Do you mind if I talk to her?"

His eyebrows rise. "Really?"

"Why do you say it like that?"

"Because you've never shown much interest in the kids."

I draw back, offended. That stings. "They're my nieces and nephews. I'm just not around a lot."

"Okay." He smacks me on the back. "Good luck."

Once Jed is downstairs, I knock. "Hey, Emelia, it's Uncle Xavier. Can I come in?"

There's no answer, so I twist the knob and find it locked. Jed never really lived in this house except for a short stint before college, but the younger Greenes were famous for locking each other out. I reach up above the door where the key is always kept, and the lock pops easily when I place the key in the hole and turn.

I open the door slowly and find Emelia lying on the bed with her head shoved face-first into a pillow.

"Hi, Emelia."

"Go away!" she yells and kicks her feet on the mattress.

"Babies suck, right?" I sit on the edge of the bed.

She peeks up but shoves her head back into the pillow right away.

"Did you know that my mom died too?"

"She did?"

I nod even though she's not looking at me. "Me, Uncle Cade, Uncle Fisher, Uncle Adam, and Aunt Chevelle... Grandpa is our dad, but your grandma isn't our mom."

She turns to suss me out, then sits up on the bed with the pillow in her hands. "Is that why you call her Marla?"

I nod again. I didn't figure anyone would have told her any of this yet. She's probably too young to really understand.

"I was thirteen when Grandpa started dating Grandma, and sixteen when Grandma was pregnant with Rylan. And I don't think of Rylan as anything but my brother. How do you feel about the baby in Molly's belly?"

She shrugs, hugging the pillow.

"Are you a little excited?"

"I heard they cry and go to the bathroom a lot. Like Axel and Laurie."

"Yeah, they do. When our two families merged together, I didn't always make it easy for my dad. But that was because I really missed my mom. I thought that maybe one day, I'd just forget her and Grandma would be my mom. But you know what?"

"What?"

"Grandma kept my mom alive for us. She'd let us have these days where we celebrated my mom's life. We'd remember all the good things about her. Your grandma never tried to take my mom's spot."

"Molly's my mom now," she says.

I nod. "She's great, right?"

"But now she's gonna love her new baby more than me because that baby will be hers and I'm not hers."

I feel for the kid. I struggled with the same feelings when we all moved into this big house on the hill all those years ago.

"I think you'll be amazed by how much love people have to share with others. Grandma loves me and I'm technically not hers."

She frowns.

"Did you know Uncle Cade, Uncle Fisher, Uncle Adam, or Aunt Chevelle weren't her kids biologically?"

"Biologically?"

I chuckle. "It just means you share the same genes."

"Why would you all wear the same pants?"

I smile. "Never mind. Did you know that we all had another mom, other than your grandma?"

She shakes her head. "She treats you all like you're hers."

"And how is that?"

"She hugs you. She tells you she loves you." She looks at the ceiling, deep in thought. "She tells you when you do bad things."

"That's the truth." I chuckle again. "Molly's a great mom, right? She hugs you?"

Emelia nods.

"She tells you she loves you?"

She nods again. "She braids my hair." She touches her long braid. "She always makes me pancakes on Saturday morning. With sprinkles."

"Sounds like she loves you a lot."

She smiles. "She does, but..."

I shake my head. "If this family proves anything, it's that there's no mine and yours, there's just *ours*."

Emelia smiles.

A soft knock on the door has us both turning to look. Molly is standing there, her eyes solely on Emelia. "How we doing up here?"

"We're just about done, right?" I eye Emelia and she nods. "Can I have a hug?"

She crawls across the mattress and wraps her small arms around me.

"Only a mom who loves her daughter would come to make sure everything is okay," I say, and she nods into my neck. "Love you, Emelia."

"Love you, Uncle X."

I release her and she jumps off the bed and runs to Molly, hugging her around the small swell of her stomach.

"Oh, sweet girl. I'm glad you had a good talk with your uncle."

She looks up at Molly. "Did you know he's not Grandma's?"

"I did. But you can't tell the difference when people love each other, can you?"

Molly mouths thank you to me.

I'm not gonna lie, having been away from my family most of my adult life, it feels good to help out a little.

She takes Emelia's hand, and they disappear down the hall.

A couple seconds later, Clara reveals herself. She steps in and shuts the door. "Pretty nice thing you did." She flips the lock.

"What are you doing?"

She walks toward me. "One thing you should probably know about me is that it gets me hot when men are vulnerable with children."

"Is that so?" I grin at her.

She nods, her eyes never leaving mine.

Once she's close enough, I swing my arm around her waist and pull her toward me. She laughs, but I swallow her laughter with a kiss. Things get a little carried away and I turn her, lowering her to the bed. I cover her body with mine, loving the feeling of having her underneath me. My hand slips under her sweater, grazing her soft skin to her breast that's covered in a silk bra. My fingers slide under the cup, brushing over her nipple.

The sound of a key in the lock surprises us and we have no time to bolt apart before the door opens to reveal Nikki. "Oh, sorry. I thought Emelia was still in here sulking. I was gonna try to cheer her up." She shuts the door.

A few seconds later, Nikki yells down to everyone, "Xavier and Clara sitting in Posey's room K-I-S-S-I-N-G." She laughs.

"I guess we're out," I say to Clara.

"I guess so."

I give her one more kiss before I help her up, because I know my family is sure to bombard us any second. "Let's go deal with the aftermath of Nikki's announcement. It's sure to be intense."

Chapter Eighteen

Clara

Xavier wasn't kidding about his family. Nikki's announcement had all the women swarming us when we returned downstairs, as if she'd told them an octopus had given birth to a whale or something absurd. There's only one person who doesn't seem on board—Presley.

Later that night, I push aside thoughts of my sister and concentrate on Xavier. He's on my couch and his legs are stretched out on the coffee table, the remote in his hand. How many times have we done this before? But tonight, it feels different.

I put a slice of apple pie on a plate and walk over to join him. We're supposed to watch Netflix. "Do you want anything?"

"Nah, I'm good." He eyes my pie and smiles. "You and your sweets."

I shrug and sit on the other side of the couch.

He pats the spot next to him. "There's no more cushion between us." I slide over and his hand rests on my thigh. "What'll it be? Documentary, movie, or a show?"

"Not a show. I don't want to feel like I'm cheating when I watch it without you."

He chuckles and squeezes my thigh. "It's all right. I'm

aware of how little willpower you have when it comes to television shows."

Last time we tried to binge-watch a show, we got through the first season, then he had to go off to training camp. I tried to act as if I hadn't watched it without him, but I'm a horrible liar.

"Okay, let's do a movie. I'd like to relax for a bit."

He looks my way and opens his mouth for a piece of pie. I fork a piece and he slides it off the fork. Again, we've done this before, but it never gave me the urge to say screw the movie, let's go spend the night in my bed.

He chews and smiles. "A movie sounds good to me."

He picks some rom-com, which I assume is because he thinks it's what he should do because that would make me happy. Which spurs me to ask a question I've been wondering about. "X? Is it weird for you?"

He pauses the movie. "Is what weird?"

"This." I eye his hand. "The affection between us now."

"Not at all. I thought it would be, but it's not." He shrugs.

"Okay." I continue eating my pie.

He dips his head. "Is it weird for you?"

"No. I mean sometimes I'm like oh, Xavier is touching me in an intimate way, but I like it."

"Clara, right now if I thought I wasn't rushing things, I'd have you up in that bedroom naked. Plus, I just want to be with you. It's really that simple for me."

I nod, wishing he didn't have to go back to San Francisco in a day.

I place my pie on the table and take the reins because it's about time I take what I want. I lift my leg and place it over his lap, straddling him and blocking his view of the TV. "I don't want to waste our night watching a rom-com."

He doesn't move, and for a moment, I second-guess my

decision. "Would you rather a documentary?" I swat his chest, and he laughs, grabbing my hands and pulling me closer. "You sure?"

"Very."

"Well then, let's continue where we left off at my parents'."

His calloused fingers and palms slide up under the hem of my sweater, and when his hands cover my breasts and squeeze them, I moan, rocking my hips side to side.

"Come here," he whispers, and once I'm close enough, his lips capture mine.

I push away all the nervous thoughts about Xavier and me having sex again and enjoy the moment instead.

His fingers slide under the cups of my bra and tug them down, causing my body to tremble with a need I'm certain he'll quench tonight. My hands explore his torso and I rest one over his heart. His thunderous heartbeat matches my own, and somehow that calms me. Maybe he's just as nervous.

His lips slip off mine and travel down my jaw. I grind against the length bulging out of his pants and arch my head back, granting him the access he wants.

"God, you're beautiful."

He tweaks my nipple with his thumb and forefinger, and my hands slide up, locking behind his neck. "Take me upstairs, X."

I moan when his hands leave my breasts, but he moves them to my ass, standing with me in his arms.

"You don't have to ask twice," he whispers. "I can't wait to be inside you again. You have no idea how many times I've relived that night between us. Tell me you're on the pill?"

"I am, and are you... I mean..."

"I'm clean. I got tested after Giulia and I haven't been with anyone since."

I hate that I have to think of Giulia or him being with her in this moment, but when he lays me on the bed and stares at me, it's clear that he's in this moment, with me.

I sit up and unbutton his pants, lowering his zipper carefully. His hand cradles my cheek, his thumb running over my bottom lip. I open my mouth and insert just the tip, as we both watch me push his pants down and palm his hard erection.

His dick twitches when I suck on the end of his thumb. "God, the things I want to do to you, woman."

I giggle, leaning forward, and pull his boxer briefs down, leaving them under his balls. I slide my tongue up his length, and his fingers tighten on my strands as a sign he likes what I'm doing. I continue to tease him, running the tip of my tongue along the head of his dick.

"I'm going to remember this forever." His voice is thick with desire.

I grab the base of his cock and position the head at my lips. I peer up at him through my long eyelashes and take him in my mouth, inch by inch until I'm deep throating him.

"Fuck." His head drops back.

I slowly draw back and pump him at the base.

"Maybe another time," he says, and his dick pops out of my mouth while he lifts me by my armpits and tosses me in the middle of the bed. "Time for you to strip."

He tears his shirt off his body and pulls his boxer briefs all the way down, leaving him completely naked in front of me. The man is a professional athlete, so his body is on point. Every bit of him is sculpted and fit.

"I want to lick you all over." I get up on my knees, but before I get a chance to get the tip of my tongue on his chest, his hands take the hem of my sweater, and he tears it off over my head. Next goes my bra, and he tosses it behind him.

"Your tits are so soft, so perfect." He cups them, the friction of the calluses on his thumbs as they run over my nipples making me moan.

"God, X." I need more, so I undo my pants myself.

"Touch yourself. I wanna watch you."

As I push my pants down to my knees, I slide my hand past the elastic waistband of my panties and slide one finger through my wet folds, lightly circling my clit. He watches with a heated gaze for a minute, his hands fondling my breasts.

It's as if a thread breaks, because he grabs the wrist of the hand down my panties and brings it up to his mouth and sucks on my fingers. Our eyes lock, and desire and need build with every swipe of his tongue until I feel as though I might combust.

Next thing I know, I'm on my back and he's tearing off the rest of what's left of my clothes. He climbs up the bed, using his thighs to open my legs wider.

"I'm gonna go mad if I don't get inside you." He situates himself between us and the tip of his dick grazes my opening.

"Please. Fuck me, X."

And that's the last of his reserve. He thrusts inside me, and my back arches from the force of it.

"So wet," he murmurs into my neck.

He thrusts and circles his hips before thrusting again. I bring my knees up to give him more space between my legs and he positions my legs so the backs of my thighs are against his chest, bending me back, and oh my god. He's so deep like this that it almost feels like too much.

"You feel so fucking perfect, Clara." He moves in and out of me at a steady pace that drives me closer and closer to my climax.

That feeling in the pit of my stomach starts, and I clench to try to hold back my orgasm as long as possible, because he's right, this is amazing, and I don't want it to end. His gaze meets mine and I lose all sense of being. Instead of him and me, it feels like an us, as though we're no longer two separate beings, but one.

As though he's reading my mind, he smiles at me, lowers my legs to his sides, and eases down, crushing my breasts under his chest. I love the heavy weight of him over me. So strong, so powerful, yet so careful not to break me. He swipes my hair away from my forehead, kissing me there and never breaking his rhythm.

The switch from intense fucking to soft lovemaking drives an emotion to the surface I'm ready for. My eyes tear up and I clutch him, never wanting to lose him again. The two years without my most trusted confidant and friend were hell.

"Hey." He draws back and wipes a tear from my cheek.

"I'm sorry. It's just... you're here. We're here. It's over." I never thought the pain would go away, but it's as if I'm watching it float into the ether above us.

"I'm never leaving you again. I promise, Clara. Never again." He kisses me and my stomach coils. "No matter what."

The slowness of his cock drawing in and out of me, hitting me at the perfect angle snaps the thread, catapulting me into an orgasm that is as full of physical pleasure as it is love. My stomach clenches as it hits me hard.

I hold him tighter, kissing his shoulder and whispering, "I missed you so much."

"I missed you too."

As I come down in the waves of my orgasm, Xavier pumps into me a few more times before he stills with a groan, then falls on top of me.

Embarrassment hits me that I basically cried while we were making love, but Xavier lifts up on his elbows and stares at me, kissing each tear as they slip from my eyes. "I mean it, Clara. You'll never be out of my life again."

"I know. I do."

"Good." He briefly kisses me once more and slides out of me, going to the bathroom.

I watch his perfect ass as he walks away, and I could pinch myself that this has finally happened, that we're here. I not only have my best friend back, but he's my lover now too. Someone must be watching out for me up there.

Chapter Nineteen

Xavier

The best part of Alaska is the winters. My teammates think I'm crazy, but on lazy days when there are limited hours of sunlight and it's snowing outside, you don't have to make up an excuse to just lie in bed. The fact that I get Clara next to me now is a bonus I didn't know I was missing.

Her hand flops over and slaps my stomach. She bolts up as if she didn't expect me to still be here. I've had to go to the bathroom for the past two hours, but I didn't want her to wake up and think I took off because I had second thoughts like last time.

Her hair is tangled, her lips swollen a delicious pink, and she's naked. Male pride stirs in my chest at the thoroughly just fucked look on her. We spent the night in bed, only going down for some snacks, and tried to watch the rom-com again in her bed, but we didn't make it very far into the movie.

"Hey," I say.

Clara laughs before her hand covers her mouth, and she abruptly stops. She throws off the covers and runs into the bathroom, slamming the door. The faucet turns on immediately.

"What are you doing?" I shout.

"Just give me ten minutes."

I stand and try the doorknob, but she's locked it. Damn, my bladder is about ready to explode. "Open the door."

"I have to at least brush my teeth."

"I've smelled your morning breath more than once in my life. I don't care. But I really have to go to the bathroom. Please open the door."

She unlocks it, standing in the doorway with a toothbrush hanging out of her mouth. Her gaze flows down my body like water. "You're naked," she mumbles around the toothbrush.

"So are you." I squeeze by her toward the toilet.

"X!"

"You want to hide things from each other? I mean, I've bought you tampons, I've held your hair when you've thrown up." I hold my dick to go to the bathroom and she leaves but doesn't shut the door. "Is that the compromise?"

I finish my business, flush, shut the lid, and wash my hands.

"We're taking it slow," she says, coming back into the bathroom.

My dick is already half chub and I place my hand on her cheek, drawing her closer to me. She finishes brushing her teeth while looking at me.

"I'll pee in private if you'd like then." I kiss the tip of her nose and grab my pants. "Tell me you have coffee?"

"Um..." She finishes her teeth brushing and joins me in the bedroom.

I toss on my shirt from last night.

"Sorry." She comes out and opens her drawers. I admire her naked body. I know every inch of it now and in just one night, I've found more than one area that gets her really hot. Imagine if I had two nights. But sadly, I have to return to San

Francisco tonight. "I ran out earlier this week and I've been at the library so much, I've been living on The Grind's."

"No problem. I'll head out and grab us some. You want a muffin too?"

"Sure. I'll just throw on some clothes and go with you."

I walk back toward her and urge her away from the drawers and over to the bed. "You're staying here, in bed, and I'll be back with coffee and breakfast in bed. I don't fly out until late, and I plan on spending all my time with you."

"Too bad I have to work," she reminds me.

My forehead falls to hers.

"But I can talk to Unessa. Maybe she'll take over for me this afternoon."

"Not if you tell her you're hanging with me." I raise my eyebrows.

"She just doesn't understand."

"Then take a shower and get ready while I get you coffee and a muffin."

"Okay." She wraps her arms around me, pressing her naked body to mine.

"Wrong move." I pick her up and deposit her on the bed, lying on top of her.

"X!"

I position myself between her legs, and when my tongue slides along the length of her folds, her objections stop. Using every one of my skills, I grin against her center when she's grabbing onto my hair and grinding onto my face.

After she's come, I leave her recovering from her orgasm and kiss her belly. "Be right back."

"You're dangerous."

I laugh, walking out of the room, down the stairs, and out of her house.

The thing about Clara's house is it's closer to town, while

my house is out on the other side of the bay. The view is great and the privacy is nice, but it's a pain in the morning when you're out of coffee.

I walk to downtown and head into The Grind, finding Zoe behind the counter. I order myself a coffee and Clara's favorite, the chai latte. Zoe stops writing for a moment, then peers up at me with a smirk. She's practically family, so I don't mind her knowing. I give her a discreet nod. Besides, with my family's big mouths, it won't be long until everyone knows anyway.

"Then you should get a morning glory muffin too, I'm assuming?"

She knows Clara as well as I do. "Yeah and I'll have—"

"Streusel, I know. It'll be right up."

I pay Zoe and wait for my order on the other side of the counter. Presley and Cade walk in with Leighton in a stroller.

"Hey, X," Cade says, nodding at me. He wheels the stroller over to me while Presley orders for them.

"She's really getting a personality, huh?" I bend down to my newest niece and pretend to tickle her stomach.

"Yeah, you caught her at a good time of day. She's happiest in the morning. We wanted to get her fresh air. Presley read some book that said for her to get used to the weather, we need to take her out in all temps. I mean, whatever." He shrugs.

"I can see that." I stand and shove my hands in my pockets.

"Looks like you're wearing the same thing you were last night?" Cade's eyebrows rise. He's my oldest brother and tends to be overprotective. We all looked up to him growing up.

"I am."

"Are you sure this is what you want?" Cade asks in a low voice, which I have a feeling comes more from Presley than him.

"Clara is what I want. I know I was a dick for the past two years, acting like some arrogant asshole with the fancy suits, limos, and model girlfriend, but I've come back down to reality. Dad being sick…"

Cade nods, probably not wanting to talk about it. Dad's illness took us all somewhere we didn't want to go. "Yeah. I gotcha on that."

Presley acts as though she's interested in watching them make the coffee, most likely so she doesn't have to talk to me. But I'm glad she's here because I need to talk to her.

"Do you mind if I talk to Presley for a moment?"

"Not sure that's a good idea. Give it some time," Cade says, making it clear where Presley stands on Clara and me.

"Presley," I say, ignoring Cade's advice.

"I said not now." Cade's voice is stronger, more authoritative now.

Presley looks at Cade, and he shrugs.

"Sure," she says.

She hands the receipt to Cade and walks over to an empty table. She sits down and looks everywhere but at me.

"I know you're worried I'm going to hurt Clara."

She huffs but says nothing.

"I'm not going to. I promise you."

Her hand goes up. "Don't promise me anything. You don't need to break both of us. No matter what, you're Cade's brother and my daughter's uncle, and I don't want to hate you for breaking a promise." She looks away from me as soon as my gaze meets hers.

"I've changed. I know you probably know about—"

"How you slept with her out of jealousy and then told

her she couldn't date anyone else even though you didn't want her? I mean, that's what you're talking about, right? How you practically pissed on her and marked your territory, then tossed her to the curb?" Her eyes are narrowed. Sometimes she and Clara look so similar you'd think they're twins.

"I made a mistake."

"A mistake that took you two years to make up for. You compounded your mistake when you bought into the media hype and acted like you were better than... strutting your model girlfriend around who probably didn't even know what position you played when you were honored at the local high school. But while you were up there smiling and acting like the world was at your feet, I was picking my sister up off the ground. You're entitled to live your life, Xavier, but when you love someone, you don't do things you know will hurt them. And if you have to, you at least talk to them about it first. Clara had come to rely on you to be there for her as a friend, and with your selfish act of sleeping with her after she told you she didn't want to if it didn't mean anything, you destroyed that. How can I be assured it's not going to happen again? Because I'm telling you right now, if you have any doubts, please walk away." Her eyes are steady on me now. "For her. If you truly love her like you say you do. Walk away if you're not one hundred and ten percent sure."

I blow out a breath and lean back in my seat. Zoe gives me a reprieve and calls my order.

I stand and pick up the coffees and muffins, then stop at Presley's table. "I'm going to prove you wrong. I'm going to make your sister the happiest she's ever been."

Presley crosses her arms and stares at me, doubt radiating off her. "For Clara's sake, I hope that's true."

I don't know Presley that well. She was new in town after I was already in the lower forty-eight playing football. Sure, Clara tells me about her and Cade, but I've never been able to get to know her myself. "I respect your opinion, Presley, I do. But Clara's belief in us is all I need."

"That's all that should matter." Her demeanor is cold.

I know it's important to Clara that her sister and I get along, but the best thing I can do is prove to her over time that she has nothing to worry about. I stand there for a second before deciding there isn't much more to say. "I better get these to her."

Cade comes over with their order.

I take the opportunity to say goodbye to Leighton. "I'll be back in a few weeks."

"Good luck with the rest of the season," Cade says and gives me a hug.

I say my goodbyes and head back to Clara's. When I come in, her phone is streaming Nikki's radio station. She's about to turn it off, but I take her in my arms, wanting to bury myself in her again. It's like now that she's mine, I can't get enough.

Nikki's voice sounds through the phone. "I just heard a rumor on my way in, Chip."

"That your brother is doing the nasty with the librarian?"

"Chip!" Nikki screeches. "We're a family-friendly show."

"It's all over the place. If they wanted to keep it hush-hush, he shouldn't have come to The Grind in the same clothes everyone saw him wearing in the pictures Marla shared on socials from your family Thanksgiving."

"Jesus, they work fast." I rest my forehead on Clara's.

"Yep, news is already out."

I shrug. "Oh well."

"Yeah." But as she slides out of my hold, I feel her shaky demeanor.

"What am I missing?"

She's quick to shake her head. "Nothing. I mean... nothing really."

"What?" I ask a second time.

"I loved last night, X. I mean, I'm in this with you, one hundred percent. And I know you mean well with the flowers and trying to hold off on our physical intimacy, but I'm still afraid of being the laughingstock of this town. Someday when I'm eighty and wheeling my scooter to the library, I don't want some parent using me as a cautionary tale and telling their kids stories about the librarian who got her heart broken by the professional football player."

"Jesus, no." I shake my head.

"I thought you wanted to keep us quiet when you didn't want me to come with you to get coffee."

"Hell no. Keeping us out of the press is one thing, but the town is something else entirely." I take her hand. "Get your coffee and muffin. I'm walking you to work so you can talk to Unessa."

She grabs all her stuff, and we walk out of her house hand in hand. All through town, we get second glances, and some people openly whisper as they pass us. I text Nikki to look out the front of the radio station so she can report what's truthful.

Once we hit the middle of the square, I spot Cade, Presley, and Leighton at an outside table of The Grind.

I stop us and put my coffee and Clara's on the nearby bench, pull up the radio station, and stream it on my phone. Then I take her in my arms. And with one hand around her waist and the other cradling her face, I kiss her, sliding my tongue between her lips. She clings to me, which is the best feeling in the world.

"And I'm watching my stepbrother, Xavier, right now kissing Clara Harrison in the middle of downtown. I do suspect this is Xavier's declaration to the town that these two are now the 'it' couple of Sunrise Bay."

When I pull back, I say quietly, "You're my girlfriend. I don't want to rush you, but I want to tell the world. You let me know when you're comfortable with that."

Her fingers graze down my cheek. "You didn't have to."

"I did. I'm not hiding us. I never will." I kiss her forehead and step back to see a smile I'd die a happy man seeing every day for the rest of my life.

Chapter Twenty

"Who doesn't love a man of mystery?"

Clara

Long-distance relationships suck.

Especially when you're heavy in the lust phase.

Even the fact that it's been full steam ahead on the extension of the library since many people in the community have been donating money hasn't helped take my mind off of Xavier.

On my way to meet Presley and Leighton at Truth or Dare, I stop to see Theo at Fired Up. He's in the studio, in the middle of sculpting something. He doesn't stop the spinning wheel thing, briefly looking up. I have no idea how he concentrates with the music so loud.

"I just wanted to stop by and say thank you for the donation to the extension."

His eyebrows crinkle as though he doesn't understand me.

"The donation online," I clarify, speaking louder over the music.

He nods and smiles, giving me a thumbs-up before concentrating on his piece of art.

After walking out, I stop by Trent Lawson's, but only his wife is there. She has stacks of papers. The bell rings when I open up the door.

"Hi, Rebecca."

"Clara. I heard the news about Xavier and you. I always knew you'd end up with him. I think your mom did too."

I can't fight my smile. My mom always did tell me that Xavier and I would find love one day, but always told me not to rush because if you get to marry your best friend, you're luckier than most. "Thank you. I just wanted to stop by. That donation to the library was way too generous."

She picks up some files, and lines on her forehead wrinkle. "Oh, that must have been Trent. He's been handling the finances since I've been up to my ears in cleaning out these files. He wanted to move to a bigger office, and I said no, we're putting some of this in storage. I'll mention to him that you stopped by."

"I appreciate that. I just didn't want it going unnoticed."

"You've always been such a sweet girl."

"Well, don't work too hard. I gotta go meet up with Presley at Truth or Dare." For a moment, I almost laugh. The first time I came face-to-face with Presley was in Trent's office down the hall.

As if she remembers too, Rebecca rounds the desk. "You two have come so far. Your mom would be so proud."

She pats my back, and although I love talking about my mom now, it still hurts that she never saw Xavier and me get together.

"See you soon."

I leave Trent Lawson's office, a little weirded out that both people I went to thank didn't seem to know what I was talking about. But it was all processed online, so they would have had to put their information in the form with their payment.

Walking across the cobblestones, I see Presley at the table nearest the wall. Cade is sitting with her as she nurses Leighton with a blanket over her shoulder. I'd be lying if I said I didn't feel a twinge of envy. I do want to be a mother, but definitely not until... oh my god, I need to stop thinking too far into the future. It's just hard when I've known him my entire life. I already know all his annoying traits.

Cade stands to greet me, leaving his chair out for me to slide into.

"Thanks, Cade," I say.

"I need to go back to work anyway. I could spend all day with these two." He kisses Presley's cheek. "Don't talk too bad about the Greene men." He winks at Presley, and she shakes her head, smiling.

"So, how are things?" I ask first.

"They're good. She's eating well, finally sleeping for five hours at night, which has been a dream. The doctor says maybe by six months, we'll have an entire night." The fact she looks anxiously eager for that to happen says she must be tired.

"I know Marla is busy with Hank, so why don't you let me take Leighton for a night? You and Cade can get away or just sleep. You can have a night or an entire weekend."

"I couldn't. It's fine. Cade helps, but I'm breastfeeding, so there's only so much he can do. One of us might as well get sleep."

We talk about bottles and pacifiers and how Leighton really did smile for real the other day. Except for the bags under her eyes, Presley looks really happy.

"Did you get our donation?" she asks, and I can't believe out of everyone, I forgot to thank her. "I'm just asking because it was weird on the form, and I wanted to make sure you got it."

"I did, and thank you very much. Too generous, as usual."

"My mom said she's going to donate too, but she better be invited to the ribbon-cutting ceremony."

"Of course she will."

Since Presley was adopted at birth, her adoptive parents still live on the East Coast. They come often to visit, but usually only in the spring and summer.

"Okay, we've made enough small talk and you've yet to speak his name. What is going on?" Presley says and removes Leighton, moves things around under the blanket, and brings her up to burp her. She does it all with finesse as though Leighton is her twelfth kid and not her first.

"It's hard. Long distance is shitty."

"Then you need to spice it up."

"By?"

"Phone sex, FaceTime sex, surely you two can figure something out."

"Are you actually Team Xavier and Clara now?"

She hasn't been shy about speaking her displeasure.

Her hand covers mine. "I just worry about you. That's all."

"Well, don't. I know Xavier better than anyone, and I trust him."

"What does he do down there when he's not busy?" That's her sly way of asking if he goes out to clubs, I bet.

"Pres, he's not going to do that."

"Hey, it's Xavier!" Cade grabs the remote and turns up the volume.

A nice-looking reporter is standing next to Xavier in the end zone. She's asking about his game this week. "Do you think you have a shot?"

"Yeah, we've got a lot on our side going in..." He talks optimistically, as he always does.

She asks him questions pertaining to Lee Burrows, the

backup quarterback, how Xavier hurt his knee the last game, but he's good as new for this game. Just as I'm about to stop paying attention—except it's so good to see his face —the reporter asks him a private question.

"I don't want to pry, but you have a lot of fans who are wondering if you're on the market? The breakup with Giulia was last year, and you were seen with her best friend, Sessilee, not that long ago. Want to fill everyone in?"

He chuckles and looks into the camera as if he knows I'm on the other side. "Thankfully, I have found a woman who took mercy on me. It isn't Sessilee though. When the time is right, you'll start seeing her pop up."

"Well, I definitely think that smile says she makes you happy."

His teeth draw over his bottom lip. "I've never been happier than with her."

The reporter looks at the camera. "There you have it. Xavier Greene is off the market. Don't cry too hard, girls, his backup would never be considered second best. Thank you, Xavier."

"You're welcome."

The news reporter shifts her attention to Lee Burrows, and Xavier walks off camera.

Presley kicks my stool, and I slide over a smidge. "What?"

"I'll give him one thing—he's owning it and he's giving you that smile. Which is the best I've seen in a long time."

I turn away because she's right. "Is it stupid to not have my wall at least half up?"

"Oh, I learned it didn't matter. When I thought I had my wall still up, it wasn't. I would have been heartbroken regardless."

"Yeah, I tried, but I just can't. I can't imagine when he comes home for off-season."

"And what about next year?" Presley asks. She seems to have a habit of asking all the questions that make me crazy.

"I'm not sure. We haven't talked about it, but if the donations keep coming in like they have been, I'm not sure what stage the extension will be at."

"Well, don't worry too much about the future. Just enjoy yourself now."

"And you'll give him a chance?" I ask. She's my sister, my only blood relative left.

"I am giving him a chance. And he's not dating me, he's dating you." She hands Leighton to me, and I rock her in my arms. "Thanks."

"He's Cade's brother, among everything else. You can't hate him."

Presley's quick to shake her head. "I don't hate him. I just worry about you. Excuse me, I have to go to the bathroom."

She leaves the table, and my phone vibrates with an incoming call. Leighton squirms as I manage to answer it with only one hand.

"Hello?"

"Hey, I just wanted to give you a heads-up," Xavier says. I hear the razzing of the players behind him. "I told a reporter that I'm off the market. I didn't give names because I won't until you're ready. I just wanted to make sure you knew."

"X, you don't have to run everything by me all the time. I know what comes with the news of me being your girlfriend."

He sounds stressed. "Other women are mean and bitchy. I don't want you to go through that. But I want to show you off to the world at the same time. Anyway. I gotta go shower.

Just didn't want you to see it and be upset I didn't say your name."

"I wouldn't be," I tell him.

"You're the best. I'll call you later, okay?"

"Okay."

I open my mouth to say something about what Presley suggested, phone sex or something, but lose my nerve.

Mandi and Nikki come in and walk toward me, then slide onto the stools to my right.

"Hey guys," I say.

"Hi. So, did you see his interview?" Nikki asks.

"Do you all have something hooked up that the minute he's on the television, you know?"

They both laugh. "Our mom was with Hank at the doctor, they were waiting, and it came on. Of course, she tapes everything with her phone, so we all got a clip."

I forgot how involved they all are in each other's lives. I've always been Xavier's friend, slightly on the outside but still a part of them. Never had to worry about being gossip with them.

"Anyway, he looked stressed," Nikki says.

"I kind of agree." Here I am, loose and carefree, smiling at everyone as if it's my birthday or something, and he's upset in San Francisco.

"You should go to him this weekend," Mandi says. "Unessa can cover for you."

"She actually can't. We're not going to see one another until he comes home for off-season."

"Then you better find a way to work him out while he's away. You know once..." Nikki lowers her voice. "Logan went away for a week to go help some guy train in the Rockies or something." She flips her hand as though it doesn't matter. "I was so horny because I was pregnant and in that second-trimester sex-crazy phase. He ended up sending me something sexy and we had sex over FaceTime."

"That's a hot idea," Mandi says.

Presley returns, picks up Leighton out of my arms, and puts her in the stroller before rocking it back and forth. "What are we talking about?"

"Unconventional sex," Nikki says.

"Talk about interesting sex things when you have babies."

"Please, you two were going at it with Leighton right there," I say.

Nikki raises her hand for a high five.

"Seriously, think about it," Nikki says.

"I will, but more importantly I want to know why I keep seeing a hot lumberjack kind of guy hanging around the Sunbay Inn?" I say. All of our eyes land on Mandi's.

Her cheeks turn bright red. "It's nothing. It's just... I don't know. He stays there sometimes when he's on assignment."

"But if he's Midge's grandson, he lives in Greywall?"

Mandi holds up her hands. "I don't know. I really don't. Family drama or something. But he's been staying at the inn for a while now, before I even knew he was Midge's grandson."

"Who doesn't love a man of mystery?" Nikki says. "It wasn't that long ago that we had a woman of mystery come to our town. Now she's our sister-in-law and married to our stepbrother."

They look at Presley and laugh.

I love my town and my life here, but the question Presley asked pops up in my mind again. What happens when Xavier goes back to San Francisco for his season? Because I can't leave the library or all my people.

Chapter Twenty-one

Xavier

I arrive back at our condo building with Ben after a grueling practice the coaches put us through after our loss last weekend.

"How are things with Clara?" he asks.

I haven't been forthcoming with him on a lot because I don't want to rub salt in his wounds, plus I don't want him to accidentally tell anyone about Clara either. "They're good."

"You know you can talk to me about her. It's not like I loved the girl or anything."

"Mr. Greene, one moment, a package came for you." Kerbie digs behind his desk.

I turn my attention back to Ben. "I don't want anyone to know about her yet. She's not used to the press."

He shakes his head. "You gotta get over that. She's a big girl."

Kerbie hands me the package.

"Thank you." I try to see who it's from, but there's no return address.

Ben and I walk into the elevator. "And don't think the guys don't notice how you never go out anymore. They're all taking bets on whether it's Sessilee or if you're back with Giulia."

"Well, I'm sure during the off-season, something will

come out." As long as no one in the media is questioning whether it's one of those two women I couldn't care less.

The elevator stops on Ben's floor, and we say our good-byes. After I ride it up to my floor and open the door to my penthouse, I place the package on the counter.

Lately, I hate how lonely coming home feels. Not that I've ever come home to anyone, but picturing Clara here waiting for me makes me wish I could. I worry I can't even live with someone else because I know I can be difficult and set in my ways.

I grab my phone and head to the couch. As always, Clara answers on the first ring.

"How was practice?" she asks. "Are you sore?"

"I wish I had you here to massage me if that's what you're asking."

She chuckles. "Oh, I do too. I kind of wish you were here with me actually, because I have the start of a cold."

"Shit, babe, I'm sorry."

She sneezes.

"Bless you. I hate this distance thing," I say for what is probably the millionth time since we started this relationship.

"Me too. Hey, you should've gotten a package in the mail. It says it was delivered."

I bolt up in my seat. "It's from you? I thought it was something from a sponsor because there was no return address on it."

"No, it's from me." I can hear the smile in her voice.

"Okay, let me get up and open it."

I grab the package, return back to the couch and rip it open. Inside I open up the plastic and pull out a small piece of fabric.

"Clara?"

"Yeah?"

"Are you sure you got this for *me*?" I look at the underwear again, turning it around.

"Okay, I know this so isn't me, but I figured it would be fun. I'm going to put something on too and we can Face-Time one another. Maybe get turned on and have a little video sex?"

"And these are gonna turn you on?" I still don't see why she would find these sexy, but I guess I never knew her kinks. Maybe this is her thing; she likes to role-play or something. I can't deny that I like her opening up to me.

"Yeah. I mean, you could be naked, but I thought this would be more fun. So, let's hang up, change, and I'll Face-Time you when I'm ready." The excitement in her tone is already getting my cock to half-mast.

"Sounds good. Don't take too long. I don't need any lingerie to get turned on when it comes to you."

"Flattering. Call you in a bit."

She hangs up and I dig in the box and find two more underwear outfits. Holding them up, I can't believe she's into this. If anything ever came out about this, I'd be the laughingstock of the team.

I double-check my front door is locked before heading to my bedroom.

I strip down and put on the underwear, checking myself out in my full-length mirror and positioning everything so it looks right. I tilt my head right and left, still completely baffled but go and lie down on the bed. I've never had video sex before and I'm thankful it's Clara I'm having it with for the first time.

My phone rings about ten minutes later with a Face-Time call from Clara. She's dressed in a red velvet top with white fur as though she's Santa. Her hair is down and flows over her shoulders. I want to crawl through the phone and fuck her.

"Damn, Clara."

She puts herself in full view using the reflection of the full-length mirror in her bedroom. "It's almost Christmas. But don't worry, this isn't your gift. Show me yours."

I lick my lips, not wanting to take my gaze away from her.

"X?"

"Sorry. Okay." I stand and go to the mirror and turn my phone to show her. "Here you go." I pretend to model, feeling a little like an idiot.

She sputters out a laugh, falling over at her waist as if she can't hold it in. "What is that? An elephant?"

"Yeah, this is what you sent me." I flop the ears on either side of my shaft that's the makeshift elephant's trunk.

"Oh my god." She's still laughing. "Where did you get that?"

I swear she's trying to zoom in.

My forehead wrinkles. "I told you, you sent them to me."

"No. I sent you a cute pair of Santa underwear that would show off your package as my present."

My free hand rises to my side. "Well, this is what came." Thank God she doesn't have a kink for this sort of thing. "I'm taking them off."

"No!" she shouts. "They're fun."

"If you think these are fun, wait until you see the other two that came in the package."

"Better than the elephant?" She coughs and laughs at the same time.

"Oh yeah. Hold up." I place the phone on my bed and change into the clown one. It has suspenders, a giant bow tie around the neck, and right at the end of my dick is a big red nose. "Ready?"

"Please." I show her the clown and she tries to reach out as though she can touch me. "We are so playing with these when you get home." The word home coming from her mouth sounds really nice right now. "I want to squeeze the nose."

"I would prefer you suck on it."

She can't control her fit of laughter. "That too. So, what's the third?"

"Funny enough, it's fitting. Hold up." I place the phone back on the bed.

"I wish I would've seen these on the site. I wonder what else they have."

"Be careful, because I'm sure I'll be able to find some crazy sexy items for you to model for me."

"I'm game," she says, and I make a mental note to buy her something.

I change into the nurse one that comes with a hat, and it might be a size too small because it takes me a while to get my package into the little area they supply for it.

"Ready?" I ask.

"As ever."

"Nurse Greene is ready to see you now." I turn the phone for her to see me, and she falls back on her bed, laughing so hard she coughs again.

"Hold on, I need water." She bends down, and with the way the phone is positioned, her tits fall forward and I get a good view of her cleavage.

"Damn, I want you here with me."

She coughs again. "Me too. I want to play in person. Especially with your new outfits."

"Where did you order this stuff anyway?" I lie down on the bed.

"Just an online store. I don't remember seeing those items, but I can't deny I'm sort of happy they messed up the order. That was hilarious." She lies on her bed, but her nose is red, and she looks as if she's about to fall asleep.

"You look exhausted."

"Nope. You're not getting out of this. Treat me like your patient." She pretends to be into it, even her smile is convincing, but I know when I'm sick, the last thing I want to do is something like this.

"I say we do this another time. You need some TLC."

"I'm fine. It's just a cold. Come on, where do I need to touch to feel better?"

"You need to get under your covers first."

"Okay." She does as I say because she's never done this before. "I'm under."

"Now take off the bra and panty set."

"But you can't see me?" She looks quizzically at me through the screen, and I laugh.

"That's the point." I glance down at my dick that's pointing north. If I saw her naked, there'd probably be precum oozing out.

The two garments come out and she puts them on the bed.

"Now turn off the lights," I say.

"You want me to put on the flashlight?"

"No, babe, go get some sleep."

She shakes her head, but she closes her eyes—probably because she's so tired.

"I promise we'll have our fun in person as soon as you're healthy."

"I hate this. I wish you were here with me." She starts to lose the fight, her eyelids slipping down.

"Dream of me."

"I will. I love you." The phone slips out of her hand, and it drops to the mattress.

"Love you, babe." I hang up and go back to the mirror to stare at myself in this ridiculous nurse outfit.

I can't help myself, I laugh just thinking about it all.

After stripping off the novelty underwear, I put on a pair of sweats and head into my kitchen to find something to eat for dinner. Nothing looks good, so I check out the delivery menus and find chicken noodle soup listed at one of my favorite restaurants.

I'm fucking Xavier Greene, I should be able to go home when I want to. Screw this. I call up and order two takeouts, then I call and charter a private jet from a company I've used a handful of times in the past—mostly when I was showboating around with Guilia.

I jog into my bedroom and pack an overnight bag, but see the men's sexy underwear on the bed. "If only for laughs."

I toss them in and change into jeans and a sweater, grab my coat, and I'm out the door to the airport. An hour later, I'm on a plane headed toward Anchorage, Alaska.

"Hold on, baby, I'm coming to nurse you back to health."

Chapter Twenty-two

Clara

I wake up drenched in sweat, my sheets as soaked as I am, but I feel a lot better.

BANG.

I startle and bolt up from my bed, listening. Someone's trying to get into my house. I tiptoe out of bed and look out the window, but there's no car in front of my house.

The doorknob jiggles again. This time I hear whoever it is put something in the lock, as if they're trying to break in. I search my room for anything to hit them with. I knew I should've adopted one of Cam's dog's puppies.

I pick up my cell phone from on top of the mattress and see that it's dead. I need to get to the kitchen for a knife before they can get in. I lightly walk down the stairs on my toes, each step gentle so they don't squeak. Whoever it is gets the door open and I catapult myself from the stairs to my couch. There's no way they'll see me from here. If they go upstairs, I can round the couch and head to the kitchen for a knife.

A bag drops and the door shuts, the lock clicking. What kind of thief locks themself in the house?

A flashlight shines through the room, and a male voice groans. I hear him open my fridge and crack open a water bottle.

I peek over the couch. What the hell?

I turn on the light and Xavier jumps into a karate pose.

"What are you doing here? You scared me shitless," I say.

"You scared me." He relaxes, taking a deep breath.

"Hello, this is my house and you're supposed to be in San Francisco."

He tilts his head and walks over, looking up and over the back of the couch. "Please greet me this way every day when we live together." His gaze soaks in my naked body.

"Don't come close, I'm sick and I just sweated off my fever." I put out my hand, but he comes over to the couch, taking me until he's next to me.

"If your fever's broken, it means you're not contagious." I sneeze right on him, and he looks at his shirt. "Good thing I grew up from that 'girls have cooties' stage."

He leans forward to kiss me, and I turn my head at the last moment, giving him my cheek.

"I did not travel this far for your cheek." He places his finger and thumb on my chin and draws me toward him, placing a light kiss on my lips. "I have chicken soup. You want it now?"

"You brought me chicken noodle soup?"

"It's the best. Remember when I was really sick a few years ago? I swear it got me healthy in, like, a day."

I laugh. "You flew all the way here just to give me chicken noodle soup?" No one has ever gone to that much trouble for me.

He shrugs. "I have to admit, I selfishly wanted to see you."

"But practice. You won't be back in time. Won't you be fined?"

"Maybe. But I'm saying I had an emergency."

My head falls back so I'm staring at the ceiling. "You don't have an emergency."

He slides closer to me. "My girlfriend is sick and it's my job to get her healthy again."

Although I feel guilt, it's one of the most thoughtful things anyone has ever done for me. "Thank you."

"You don't have to thank me." He slides his arms under my ass and arms. "But you do have to go to bed." He carries me upstairs.

"Tell me the elephant is under the jeans?"

"Sorry, but if you get healthy, I might've packed them. All depends on whether you get better before I leave."

As he's about to drop me on the sheets, I remember how wet they are. "The sheets, I sweated out my fever."

"Does that mean you need to shower? Jeez, talk about a hard job." He winks and leaves me on the edge of the bed, going into my bathroom and turning on the shower. "And you know that I'll have to go in with you just in case you get light-headed."

I roll my eyes. "Well, if you must."

"I insist."

He gets undressed and I really wish I was healthy so I could enjoy that perfect athletic body of his.

"Which key did you use?"

"The one in the rock. I think you need to switch it out." He goes back into the bathroom. "It sticks," he shouts over the water.

"Well, it's about eighty years old. Why didn't you use your key?"

He stands in the doorway, naked and uncaring. "I put it away when we were fighting, and I didn't want to use it until I felt sure you'd want me to."

I rise from the bed and walk steadily toward him, my eyes never straying from his. "Use the key, X. It's yours."

He nods. "Okay. Now shower time for my girl."

He opens my shower door and I step in, and he joins me right after. I stand under the cascade of water and my eyes close because it feels good. Then two large hands land in my hair. Suds fall down my shoulders as he threads his fingers through my long strands of blonde hair.

"Do you think you'll ever go back to being brunette again?"

"Why? Did you like me better with dark hair?"

"I don't care if you have purple hair. It's up to you." He kisses my shoulder.

After the shampoo, he piles conditioner in my hair.

"X?" I hate to broach this subject right now, but after he's done a complete one-eighty and shown up here, I feel as if I need to.

"Yeah?"

"Can I ask you a question?"

"Anything."

His fingers are like magic as he runs them against my scalp and my eyes drift closed. I'm barely able to remember what I wanted to say. "Your fears about... us... relationships... they seemed to have disappeared and I just wondered as your best friend, not your girlfriend." I turn around in his arms and he holds me close. "Are you really doing okay? We've moved so fast."

He walks his fingers up and down my spine. "Honestly?"

"Always. Please never tell me something just because you think I want to hear it."

"I'm *so* happy. Sometimes I'm pissed that I never allowed us to cross that line before. How was I so blind not to see you in that way? I guess I finally realized that if I sat back and stayed scared, I'd never have moments like these with you. I just had to push past the fear, and what's on the other side is life changing. I can't predict the future, but I want to spend as many days making memories with you as possible, regardless of what the future brings."

"Really?"

"Really." He kisses my forehead. "How about you?"

"I feel the same—happy. I get mad sometimes too that we waited so long, but maybe the timing wasn't right back then. Sometimes I wonder if we had been together when your dad first got sick, maybe that wouldn't have been our time. Maybe you would've doubled down on your fears, you know?"

He backs me into the shower spray to rinse out my conditioner. "I know exactly what you're saying, and unfortunately, I think you might be right. There is one more thing I want to talk to you about."

"What?" I close my eyes as the water washes down my head.

"Coming out. I have some red-carpet events coming up, and when we're out together, people will assume I'm bringing my best friend, Clara. If I announce that you're my girlfriend, there are gonna be haters. Virtual bullies who type whatever they want without considering the repercussions. Mean-spirited people."

"You forget how long I've been in this world with you. I can handle it."

He nods and I see the concern in his eyes. "It scares me. Because I'm public, people take it as me and anyone in my life are open game."

"I'll be fine. Plus, I live up here. It's not like I'm down in San Francisco."

He looks down his nose at me. "Social media is everywhere."

"I know." I wrap my arms around his neck, loving the feel of our wet, naked bodies pressed together. "I'm fully aware of what's coming my way, but you're worth it, Xavier."

He sighs. "I really hope you feel that way."

I pick up the loofah and soap. "Time for you to wash me."

"Yes, ma'am."

Xavier soaps my entire body, taking longer in some spots than others. Once I'm done, we step out and he wraps a towel around me.

"Now sit in this warm bathroom until I say it's time to come out."

"I'm good." I cough.

He leaves, shutting the door. I'm not sure how much time passes before he comes back in and brings me over to the bed. A pair of pajamas have been laid out, and he grabs my brush on the way out of the bathroom.

"You don't want me naked?"

"I want you comfortable and warm. Put on the pajamas and let me brush out your hair."

"I feel like I'm at a sleepover. Don't freeze my bra."

He shakes his head, but I see him opening his bag.

"Are the goods in there?"

"Sure are."

"Put one on for me. Please?" I whine.

"No way. You won't be able to keep your hands off of me."

I laugh, which turns into coughing, which turns into choking. Xavier raises his eyebrows.

My shoulders sink. I know I need more rest, so I dress in

the warm pajamas I usually wear during the winter when I'm alone in bed. I slip under the fresh sheets Xavier put on the bed, and he comes up behind me and brushes my hair.

"Remember when you tried to teach me how to braid?" he says, amusement in his tone.

"I do. You'd always complain."

"Because I wanted to play in the treehouse or play football."

That was when our friendship took a turn for a brief moment when we were around twelve. He could play with his friends, and I could do girly things like learning makeup and braiding. We would still get together, but there were fewer times back then.

"What do you think our moms would say if they saw us now?" I ask.

He secures my wet hair in a ponytail. "I think they'd be really happy for us."

"Yeah, same. I wish they could see it, you know?" I feel myself getting choked up. I don't want to ruin tonight with tears.

"They see it," he says and kisses my shoulder. "Now go to bed, baby."

He opens up the comforter some more and gets in. His big body behind me gives me the same safe and secure feeling I've always had with him.

"Thank you for coming. I hope you don't get in trouble," I say, putting my head on the pillow.

His arm slides around my stomach as if we're not close enough. "You're worth any trouble I might get into. This is where I'm supposed to be. Now sleep."

I chuckle and rest so much easier when he's with me.

Along with the joy in my heart, I can't help but think

something bad is going to happen. That maybe we're *too* happy. That everything is too simple. *Stop it, Clara, you've been through hell and it's your time to be happy.* I tell myself this over and over until I drift away.

Chapter Twenty-three

Xavier

Finally, my football season is done. I feel like a slacker, because toward the end, I think a part of me was somehow hoping we wouldn't make the playoffs. But we had a lot of issues with our offense this year, and even if we had squeaked into the playoffs, we probably wouldn't have made it past one round. I feel good about my own game this year though. Still, losing stings. But this just wasn't our season. I've been in this business long enough to know that some years, no matter how hard you work, how much you put into it, it just doesn't come together the way you want.

I drive into Sunrise Bay a day earlier than I'm supposed to and it feels like a breath of fresh air. This isn't just a one-night visit, I'm back for months. Months I get to spend with Clara. *In* Clara. She still thinks I'm coming back tomorrow, so I'm surprising her at the library.

My Uber driver drops me off outside the library and I sneak in, hoping no one sees me and sends her a text telling her I'm back, ruining the surprise.

Unfortunately, Unessa is at the front counter. She's dyed her hair jet black, and she still has a look of disdain on her face when she sees me.

"Hey, Unessa."

"Couldn't make the playoffs, huh? I thought you were this famous quarterback no one can top?"

I chuckle. "It was a tough season, but thanks for following." I wink.

She scoffs. "I'm not following your career. I just figured all the good teams are still playing and here you are back in your hometown."

My jaw tics. "How about you just tell me where Clara is?"

"Clara is in her office if you must know." She continues to scan in books.

"Thanks, Unessa. I like the hair by the way."

"Don't be condescending," she says to my back because I'm already past her.

I get ten steps away before I hear my name.

"Xavier!" Grandma Ethel shouts from behind me.

A few people shush her.

"Oh please, get a life," she says to the complainers.

I turn around to find her, Dori, and Midge standing there with piles of books in their hands. "Hey, Grandma." I kiss her cheek. "Dori. Midge." I give them each a nod. "Sorry, I gotta go."

"This is so perfect. Clara is coming over to Northern Lights tonight—"

I whip back around. "I'm sorry, what?" I must not have heard her correctly. After months of a long-distance relationship, I'm back and she's telling me my girlfriend is spending the evening at the old folks' home? "Why is she going there?"

"She's reading us some excerpts from books." She nods at the piles of books in their hands.

"You can all read, why does she have to read to you?" I

ask impolitely. I'm surprised my grandma hasn't smacked me on the head by now.

"Because some of us have cataracts and the font is small. But now that you're back early, you can come too. You two could act it out."

I stare blankly because Grandma better be joking. "Act out an entire book?"

"No. We're picking out excerpts to compare and contrast," Dori fills me in.

I glance at the books. From the covers, they look like romance. "What are you comparing and contrasting?"

"The poetry of the words, of course," Grandma says.

"I think you should all read the passages yourselves." From the look on Grandma's face, I picked the wrong thing to say. "Just give me a moment to say hello to Clara. She doesn't know I came home early. It's a surprise. You know, so we could spend the night together." I turn to walk to her office.

"We'll be right here waiting for you."

I give her a wave, not turning around. Clara's office is in the back of the library, next to the bathrooms, which we've made plenty of jokes about through the years. I slide in the office door and shut it behind me, locking it so the grandmas don't come in.

She looks up and screeches. "X? You're here?"

"I am."

I don't wait. She stands and I round her desk, taking her into my arms, pressing my lips to hers, and kissing her so hard she feels how much I've been thinking about doing this for weeks. I close the kiss before we get too carried away, knowing we can't go any further with the three grandmas in the library.

"Oh, I missed you." She stares up at me with that look I can't get enough of, as if I'm her everything.

"Me too, but we have a problem. I was all set to dress up as a clown or elephant tonight, but I hear you're reading them romance at Northern Lights?"

She laughs. A full belly laugh. "Well, I'm sure some of them would enjoy it if you dressed up."

I put my hands on my hips, staring at her.

"I'm sorry, but you weren't supposed to be home until tomorrow. But now you can come with me."

"They want me to act out the scenes with you. From a romance book."

"Romance? They told me I was reading the facts of Lake Starlight and how it became a city and what it's known for. And if we have time, we would do Sunrise Bay and Grey-wall. No one said anything about romance. I'm not doing that."

"Well, they're hanging out there picking out books for the two of us to act out."

She walks by me, and I stare at her ass, happy that I'm not saying goodbye to it anytime soon. Opening the door, she storms down the hall.

The three grandmas are at a table, laughing and carrying on with the books open in front of them. Clara stops about ten feet away from them.

I come up alongside her. "Want me to tell them?"

The minute her shoulders fall, I know the answer. "They look so happy. If they want me to read a few romance excerpts, so be it."

"You're too nice."

She turns and kisses me on the cheek. "Get ready, because you're coming with me. Welcome home, X." She saunters back to her office.

How did my night go from screwing to getting screwed over?

CLARA and I arrive at Northern Lights Retirement Center, and I hold her hand on the way in.

LeeAnn, the coordinator of these events, stands when we walk in. "You guys have a full house today."

"You took all phones away?" I ask. The last thing I need on the internet is a recording of me reading a sexy excerpt from a romance book in a retirement home.

"Yes. I told them they'll get them back when you guys are done. But you know they can be..."

"Sneaky? I know." I sigh and glance at Clara.

I've been speaking my displeasure about this, but I can't complain too much because when Clara got home, she showed me how happy she was that I was home in Sunrise Bay by falling to her knees. And of course, being the gentleman I am, I returned the gesture in kind. She thinks she fooled me, but I know it was to make me happy. And it worked.

"Come on, I'll introduce you guys."

We walk into the library at the retirement center and LeeAnn wasn't joking. There are walkers, wheelchairs, and every chair that's been brought in is filled. My grandma and her groupies are in the front row. There's a table set off to the side with some refreshments and food and I can't help but notice a platter of cookies that look similar to the ones from the bakery in Lake Starlight I love that arrived at my condo unexpectedly. Figures.

"Quiet down, everyone, please, our guests have arrived," LeeAnn says.

The three of us make our way to the front. Grandma is beaming at me as if I made her night, and Clara's right. Who am I to deny them this? She's done more than she had to for me by locking me in Terra and Mare with Clara and forcing us to take the first step toward reconciliation. If not for that, maybe we wouldn't be here.

"This is Xavier Greene, Ethel's grandson, and his girl-friend, Clara Harrison, the town librarian in Sunrise Bay. Ethel, Dori, and Midge have picked out some excerpts from some books that they'll be reading to you."

A hand in the back shoots up.

"Yes, Dottie?"

"I heard they're romance books?"

"Only one or two," LeeAnn says. "We have some others about World War Two and cooking. We can't take up all their time, so we picked about five books."

"I understand that, LeeAnn, but there is a romance book in there, right?" Dottie sounds a little annoyed.

I grab Clara's hand. She smiles at me, and that nonverbal communication we used to have so fluidly is there again.

"Yes. Now let's all quiet down and let them get started."

There are two chairs at a table that's stacked with more than five books. I look at Grandma and she only grins, as if she's not the reason there are more than five sitting there.

"Please go ahead. I think I'm going to stick around for this one just in case." LeeAnn goes to the back and leans against a table.

Clara waves. "Hi, everyone! We're thrilled to be here. Reading is a really important activity to keep the mind sharp and—"

"Let's get to the reading," a man calls.

Clara glances back at me.

"Ronnie!" LeeAnn scolds.

"Okay... maybe we'll just dig in." Clara sits down and I sit next to her.

She picks up the first book, which is about two women writing letters to one another during the war. It seems to be mostly about the friendship they grew even though they were in different stages of their lives.

Once Clara's done, I read from a book about Italian food and the heritage of the ingredients. We breeze through, and it's an hour before we're done with all of the books but the romance one. It sits on the table like a scorpion, ready to strike, and neither of us wants to pick it up.

"You two do it together," Dori says, waving her finger back and forth between us.

"Um..." Clara looks at me.

"If it gets us out of here, let's just do it," I whisper and pick up the book. Clearing my throat, I hold the book out between us. I scan the page briefly and look at Clara. "I can't read this out loud."

"Let's just get it over with." She takes the book, and her jaw hangs open. "Who picked this book?"

Midge raises her hand.

"Um..."

"Oh, come on. It's okay to be kinky every now and again, Clara," Midge says.

I open my mouth to say something, but Clara's hand lands on my thigh under the table. "Okay, here we go. Don't say I didn't warn you all." Clara starts reading.

"How about I relax you before we head out? I know you hate these things," she whispers, her hand sliding between our bodies and palming my hard dick.

Clara holds the book out for me to read.

"No objections there." I lean back on my arms, and she kisses

me on the lips, sliding her tongue into my mouth before descending down my body.

I help her pull down my track pants since I've yet to get ready. My dick springs out as soon as she pulls down the elastic waist to rest under my balls.

I feel my face heating the further we get into this.

"This image is going to be burned into my brain," I say, watching her grasp the base of my dick and direct the tip to her luscious lips. She slides her tongue out and twirls it around the tip, and it takes all my control not to lift my ass up and push past her plump lips. "Fuck, Gen."

She continues to use her mouth on my cock while locking her gaze with mine. It's all I can do not to come when she takes me as far back in her throat as she can, then slides back up, her tongue taking over while her fist jerks me off.

"Come here," I say, attempting to get her up, but she shakes her head.

Okay, that's enough for me. I pass the book back to Clara to take over.

"I'm the boss this time."

Chuckling, I put both hands out to my sides. "You will be fucking me with that jersey on later though."

"Deal."

She finishes and we shut the book.

"Okay, we're done for the evening. It's been so much fun." I get up and hold my hand out for Clara's.

"Yeah, I gotta go to the bathroom." A man stands and walks by us with an erection tenting his pants. "Thank you two. Very enlightening."

"Damn it, Earl." Grandma pretends to cover her eyes.

What did she think was going to happen?

"Meet me in my room," Earl whispers to Midge way too loud for it to be a secret.

"Oh my!" a woman in the back says, fanning herself.

LeeAnn walks up from the back to address the group. "Now I want to say that whoever chose this specific excerpt, it was very sexual. But most people read romance books for the love and heartfelt emotion. A couple finding their way together and falling in love."

"I like the ones where they tie one another up," a woman in the back says.

"Not me. I don't like to read about the sex, just the relationship," another says.

Clara smiles at them both. "That's the great thing about reading, there are different books for everyone. How about I bring a few by that will suit all your reading needs?"

LeeAnn pats Clara's shoulder. "That would be great. Let's thank Clara and Xavier for coming tonight."

A phone rings in the distance and LeeAnn leaves to go answer it, I assume.

"Which one is Fabio on?" a man calls.

"He's not really on covers anymore, but I might be able to find one," Clara says.

"There's a twenty in it for you if you bring us that one with the red room," another man says.

A woman with a walker stands in the back. "Am I the only one who thinks we're asking for disaster by bringing romance books in here?"

A few people grumble and I look at Clara, silently begging her to get us the hell out of here.

"Sit down, Rita. You're such a prude." Midge waves her hand at her.

"I'd rather be a prude than the center slut."

All three of the grandmas stand, albeit slowly. Grandma and Dori look ready to defend their friend.

"Now, ladies," Clara says, stepping forward.

I've never seen this aggressive side of them, but the three grandmas wind through the room until they're in front of Rita.

"Do something," Clara whispers to me.

I slide past all the chairs until I'm between them.

"Say it to my face," Midge says.

"Everyone knows you like the sex," Rita huffs.

"There's nothing wrong with sex." Midge points in her direction, and if I wasn't between them, I think her finger would've pressed into Rita's chest.

I glance at the doorway. Where the hell is LeeAnn?

"Please, the other day I saw Earl wearing this ridiculous clown underwear outfit and you kept saying, 'Let me honk your red nose.'"

My mouth drops open and I look at Clara across the room. This has to be a coincidence.

Before I can brace myself or see it coming, a huge bag smacks me across the face.

"That's my grandson!" my grandma screams at Rita, as I find my way to a chair.

Clara rushes over and situates herself between my legs, staring at my cheek. "Oh, X." She's laughing hysterically.

I knew tonight was a bad idea.

Chapter Twenty-four

Clara

Xavier has been home for a month, and we've found our new normal. Mostly we spend time at my place, but tonight he asked me to come to his house.

I drive out to the other side of the bay, closer to where Adam and Lucy live, and park in his driveway in front of his house.

Xavier bought the land and built his house years ago knowing he'd be spending the majority of his downtime in Sunrise Bay. It's a four-bedroom, three-bath, gorgeous home and everything is new. Should things move forward with us, it would make sense for us to live here, but I love my childhood home and the fact that it's close to town.

I open the door and knock. "X?"

"In the kitchen."

I follow the smell of dinner, and there in the kitchen is Xavier, hard at work. He's got his apron on and his hair is styled, making him the most handsome man ever. But I could be biased.

"Come kiss the chef," he says.

I walk over and run my hands up his rigid torso until I rise on my tiptoes and place a kiss on his lips. "What are you making us?"

"Just some salmon, potatoes, and green beans. Nothing

special, but if you eat all your veggies, I have a surprise dessert for you."

"Oooh, yummy."

He pours a glass of wine and hands it to me.

"I hate to say this, but I hope it's not the clown outfit. I'm not sure I can handle that," I say.

"Yeah, I can't either, but you want to know something funny? Kerbie mailed me a package that came to the condo. It's on the table."

I head over to the table and, sure enough, it's the Santa underwear I sent him. I hold them up. "So, do you think…"

"No, I'm going with it just being a screwup. No way my grandma sent me elephant underwear." He turns back to what he's working on, wineglass in hand.

I raise my eyebrows like, don't be so sure, then look around. There are candles lit on the table with plates and forks all laid out. "So, this is like a date night?"

"Yep, and I have something to talk to you about."

I still, and the room is silent.

Xavier laughs. "Nothing like that. I got a call today and there's a magazine that wants to do an article on me." He turns around and his teeth skate across his bottom lip.

"What kind of article?" I meet him back in the kitchen, propping myself up on the counter.

He holds up a potato for me and I wrap my lips around the fork tongs. I nod that it's done, and he turns off the burner.

"Finding love while playing the game." He plates our dishes and carries them to the table. "Which means you're a big portion of that article."

"I would hope so."

He chuckles and steps between my legs. "So, what do you think? Want to go public?"

I run my hands through his hair. "You know I'm not the one who shied away from it. It was you."

"I'm still scared. I never want you to be hurt, and some of these people are brutal. My first year as starter, I wanted to crawl into a hole."

"And now look at you."

"People are still mean, I just stopped reading the comments. They're never happy and of course, they can always do a better job than me." He rolls his eyes. He tips his forehead down, so it meets mine.

"I think you're amazing. I mean, look how far you've come. It's a story most guys dream of."

His hands tighten on my ass. "This is what people dream of. Finding their one and only. So?"

"Of course I'll do it."

"Great. Although I hate that we're stuck in this position because of my job, I do want everyone to know I'm yours and you're mine."

He picks me up, and I wrap my legs around his waist, my hands working on the apron tie behind his neck. "You should be naked."

"Next time." He kisses me and carries me to the chair, then drops me there before taking off the apron and sitting down too. He clicks the remote sitting by his dish and romantic music comes on through the speakers while we eat.

A true date night with the love of my life. How perfect can our life be right now?

TWO DAYS LATER, I'm walking through town, thanking everyone for all the donations we've gotten recently. It's really amazing how the townspeople have come together for this cause. I stop at Two Brothers and an Egg, and Tad is busy as ever, so I make it quick.

"Tad, I just wanted to thank you," I say while he's getting a muffin for someone.

"For what?" He looks at me, but I can tell his mind is somewhere else.

"The donation to the extension." I smile.

"Oh, did Brad already do that? I know we were talking about it. Sorry it's not as much as others. Business hasn't been as great as it's been in the past." He frowns, but the donation he made online was more than most businesses around here.

"Everything helps, and I thought it was a very generous donation."

He smiles and heads out from behind the diner counter to deliver the muffin to a table. "Anything for you, you know that. Bring your man around sometime. He hasn't shown his face since he returned."

"Ah, I think he's a little embarrassed about how his season ended. He likes to impress you."

"I'm serving omelets and pancakes. I just like to talk football with him."

I laugh. "I'll tell him."

"Bye, Clara."

I leave the diner and stop at Handyman Haven, where the gossip brigade must be having their meeting because all four of the veterans are huddled around the cash register with George, the owner. The gossip brigade is a group of veterans who I swear tell Nikki all the gossip that happens in town so she can announce it on her show.

"Hi, George." I nod toward the men. "Guys."

"Clara Harrison, to what do I owe the honor? You have a

big, strong man to be helping you with projects around the house now."

"Oh, I'm not here for that. I just wanted to thank you for your donation to the library extension."

A frown hits his face, but he recovers quickly with a smile. "You're welcome. Hopefully it does some good."

"It will. Honestly, I never expected so much help from everyone. It's been so encouraging." I can't help the megawatt smile on my face.

The gossip brigade whispers among themselves as if one has all the information the others don't.

"Well, we all love you and know you'll make it great." George is unusually chipper today.

"Yes, thanks again," I say. "I better get going."

I walk out of Handyman Haven and head down the sidewalk toward the library. At least George knew what I was talking about. Some of the reactions I've gotten when I've thanked people have been odd. I'm sure that everyone is just busy with their own lives and has stuff going on. The fact that they donated isn't on the top of their mind.

I walk into the library and a text pops up on my phone.

The interview is set for next Friday at noon. We'll be at my place.

Thanks. I'll be there.

Come back and spend the day with me in bed.

I laugh and Unessa rolls her eyes.

Some of us have to work for a living.

You don't have to work, I'll take care of you.

I let that text hang there. Please tell me that's not what he thinks will happen.

"Uh-oh, something happen with Prince Charming?" Unessa asks.

"No." I shove my phone into my purse. "Anything I need to know?"

"Nope."

"Okay, I'll be in my office for a little bit if you need me."

I walk through the library, the text at the forefront of my mind. We haven't discussed what our life might look like long term, but I really hope he doesn't think he's going to be my sugar daddy or something.

I sit at my desk, unable to concentrate. Xavier knows how important the library is to me, I know he does. And he always said when he retires, he plans to come back to Sunrise Bay. But I don't feel comfortable bringing any of this up because it's dealing with something way far into the future.

A knock on my door startles me.

"Come in," I say, pretending to be working in case it's one of the employees.

George Lehmann walks in with his head down.

"George," I say. "What can I do for you?"

"May I sit?" he asks, nodding toward the chair.

"Sure."

He sits, and a long silence commences. I give him time since he doesn't seem like the usual George, the one so sure of himself.

"I wanted to apologize. I didn't make that donation, but I didn't want to admit that in front of my friends. I'm sorry, Clara, business hasn't been as good as before. Of course I want Sunrise Bay to have a library extension, but I wasn't able to help. Maybe after tourist season, when the leasing companies are getting the rentals prepared for summer season."

The inkling that not all the people I talked to about their donations knew what I was talking about resurfaces. And Xavier's name lights up in my head in big neon letters.

"George, it's okay. But someone did make a donation in your name."

He nods. "About that. There are rumors… rumors of you thanking companies that aren't making these donations. I think someone else is making them."

I lean back in my seat. "Who do you think it is?"

"A mystery donor? In our small town?" He looks at me.

Clearly, we have the same person in mind. Only a few people here have the money to afford these donations. Logan, Nikki's husband; Gavin, Posey's fiancé; and Xavier. Since Logan and Gavin aren't originally from Sunrise Bay, nor are they dating the librarian, that leaves one person.

I stand and grab my purse. "Thank you so much, George, and I would never want to put you or anyone in a position where your financial security is at risk. So, don't think anything of it."

He stands. "What are you going to do?"

"Don't worry about it."

"No one wants to cause problems. Everyone loves you and Xavier together."

I laugh. "Don't worry about that, we'll be fine."

I walk George out and tell Unessa I'll be out for a bit. Then I walk back to my house to pick up my car and drive to Xavier's. He's not home, so I go to the one place I know he'll be—Hank's.

Chapter Twenty-five

Xavier

"He's in remission!" Marla says as soon as she opens the door for me. They were just at my dad's doctor. We embrace and Marla has tears flowing down her face. "It was a hard road, but I'm so happy we came out on the other side. We're so much more fortunate than others."

"That's amazing." I pull back and smile at her. "Can I see him?"

"He's out back. You know, back to work as expected."

"Thanks, Marla." I walk past her to go to the deck, but she calls me back. "Yeah?" I turn around.

"I just wanted to thank you for talking to Emelia. Whatever you said really made a difference. She's back to the happy girl she's always been." Tears fill her eyes. "Excited about the baby."

"I'm glad I could help." I turn to continue walking to the back of the house.

"Mind me asking what you said?" Marla asks, and I stop walking.

I slowly turn to face her. "I just told her that in this family, there's no hers or his, there's just *ours*. That I wasn't yours, but you never made me feel that way."

Another tear falls down her face. "Thank you, Xavier, that means a lot to me."

"It's the truth. Not sure where my family would be without you, Marla."

More tears run down her cheeks. "Oh, look at me. Menopause." She rushes over and grabs a Kleenex from the box.

A knock on the front door interrupts us. I wait while Marla opens it, sniffling from the tears.

Clara's standing there and takes in the scene. "What happened? Hank? Where is he? Did you get bad news?"

Her terrified expression should have me rushing to tell her no, it's good news, but I love that she's so invested in my family. As if my family is hers, which I guess it is for the most part. My dad has been a father figure to her since her dad died.

Marla shakes her head. "Hank's in remission. It's good news. These are happy tears."

"Really?" Clara beams. "*Yay!*" She rushes to Marla, hugging her tight, then pulls me in with them. The three of us are in a hug, Clara bouncing up and down. She releases us and then sets her gaze on me. "We need to talk."

A cool rush of air chills the room.

"Oh, I should leave you guys alone then." Marla walks away.

"What's up?" I ask.

I reach for her, but she steps back. "Not so fast."

"What could I have possibly done in the last two hours?"

She crosses her arms over her jacket. "I'd actually say you've been doing it for months."

Oh shit. How did she catch me? I should've known she's too smart for that.

"Babe..."

She holds up her hands. "Don't babe me. I told you I wanted the town to help with this investment back into Sunrise Bay, not have the star quarterback pay it all."

I frown. "But it's important to you."

"Yes, and so are the donations. I like the idea of the community coming together to make it happen and I don't like that you tricked me. Not to mention that I was going all over town thanking people like an idiot."

A laugh bubbles up my throat, but when I see her stern expression, I hold it back. "I never meant for you to feel that way. But the people in the town can't all contribute. My dad told me the other day that the economy hasn't been great. Mayor Klein really messed up our tourism. Gavin's working to make things better, but it's not the kind of thing you recover from in a few months or even a year. And regardless of the librarian sleeping in my bed at night, I do want to invest in my hometown. I have the means, so why stop me? Plus, think what the extension will do for the businesses in town. The people working on it will be at Handyman Haven buying tools and supplies, eating at Two Brothers and an Egg, getting their coffee fix at The Grind, having lunch at Truth and Dare, maybe buying flowers for their wives. No matter how you spin it, it's good for Sunrise Bay."

A small smile tilts her lips, and she sinks into my arms. "How did I not see any of that?"

I put my finger under her chin and lift it for her to look at me. "You've had a lot going on. Reconciling your killer friendship with a hot quarterback, and that hot quarterback has been keeping you busy late at night."

She laughs and I squeeze her into my hold, kissing the top of her head over and over.

"I'm surprised you didn't come out swinging," I say.

Her laughter vibrates in my chest. "I'm not as aggressive as I used to be."

We stay like that for a few minutes, both of us probably thinking about the time she did come over here swinging when she thought I didn't vote for her for student president. Damn rumors in high school.

"Does you being here mean you took the day off?"

She backs away from my embrace. "No. I have to go back. But I want to go congratulate Hank before I leave."

I place my hands on her face and bend down to kiss her. It's short and sweet and perfect, just like her.

We walk out to the patio, where my dad is on a ladder and Marla is yelling at him. She grows quiet when we walk out.

"Everything good?" she asks.

"Yeah," I answer. "Dad, Marla's right. Get off the ladder. I'll do it."

"I've been staring at this piece of wood on the pergola. It's going to come down and crash into one of the little ones. Spring is coming soon."

I look at all the snow still on the ground. "I'm not sure about that. Come down so Clara can congratulate you on being in remission. She's gotta go back to work."

My dad smiles at Clara and gets down off the ladder. While he's busy with Clara, Marla and I manage to take the ladder. She hauls it to the garage, laughing as if we got away with something.

"My son treating you well?" my dad asks.

"Always," Clara answers, and we share a look because that may not always have been the case, but from this day forward it is. "Congratulations. Now don't go putting your life in danger during the winter months. You need to recover from those treatments. Need another book?"

He shakes his head. "No, I'm good. Thanks, Clara."

They hug and more tears fill her eyes, but at least they're from happiness.

Of course, how could she not be thinking of how the treatments didn't work on her mom as well as they did for Hank? Then again, knowing Clara, she's just happy Hank is still here and healthy again.

"I'm going to walk Clara out, then we need to talk," I tell my dad.

He nods because he knows what I need to talk about.

"I'll get Marla," he says. "Have a great day, Clara, and if he does anything, you come to me. I'll handle him."

I roll my eyes. Clara laughs while I swing my arm around her shoulders, walking her on the shoveled path around the house to her car.

"Hurry home," I say after she opens her car door.

"Five o'clock as always, antsy pants. You might have to come up with a hobby during the off-season."

I chuckle. "Or we could be traveling all over the world..."

She stares at me extra long but kisses my lips. "Gotta go."

She slides into the car and shuts the door before starting the engine. I wave goodbye and head back into the house.

Marla already has the jewelry box on the counter when I step into the kitchen.

"Are you hungry?" she asks, taking some things out of the fridge.

"No. I just... well... I really want her to have the piece now instead of waiting until the wedding."

Marla bites her lips and looks at my dad.

I look between them to try to figure out what they're thinking, but I have no clue. "What?"

"We have something else for you. We didn't want to give

it to you until you and Clara were well... together," my dad says.

"I wanted to surprise you both with it at your wedding, but Hank thinks now that you're together, it's nice for you two to see it." Marla pours out a bag of chips with dip. The woman always wants to feed us, but sometimes I think it's her nervousness when we talk about my mother.

It's my mother's jewelry box on the counter. Each of us boys were given an item to hold on to for the woman we love.

"Just keep the bracelet handy, okay? But what's the other item?"

My dad goes into the dining room and pulls out a box. "Open it together," he instructs. "That's all I ask."

"Okay..."

"Xavier, are you thinking about proposing soon?" Marla asks the question my dad probably wants to.

"Um... I don't know. I don't want to rush her."

They both laugh and share a look.

"What?"

"Son, the two of you built a solid layer first. You built up your friendship and now you're embarking on love, but that friendship is what's going to get you through all the hard times so you can enjoy the triumphs of your love."

"I just don't want... I mean..."

"Are you not sure?" my dad asks with a frown.

"No. She's the only one, but we have one last hurdle." I sigh. "The press."

"Clara is beautiful. What could they possibly say?" Marla asks.

"It's too easy to pick on someone when you don't know them. Some of these women tore Giulia apart. Too thin, resting bitch face, the dresses she wore. How she never wore my jersey. You name it, they picked it apart. It'll happen to Clara too. Probably more if the world knows how much she means to me."

"Well, she'll do fine. She's self-confident enough to handle it."

"I know, but even I've doubted myself because of some of these assholes behind a computer. They love you when you're up and hate you when you're down. Some might even say my relationship is why the end of the season went to shit."

"You have to be secure within yourself, son," Dad says. "We've been over this several times throughout the years. You do your best out there. Everyone's a Monday morning quarterback. But they weren't drafted, they aren't playing."

I nod because I know all that. I do. I just never want anything to hurt Clara again. I want to be the one who makes her feel better, not be the reason she's unhappy in the first place.

I pick up the box. "Thanks for this. Whatever it is. It's not embarrassing pictures of us bathing together or something, right?"

"No."

I give my dad a one-arm hug. "I love you. I'm so happy you're in remission."

My dad claps me on the back. "Love you, son."

I hug Marla and leave the two of them standing in the doorway, waving. My dad's arm is around Marla's shoulders, and when I look at them, I realize I want to be them. I want that to be Clara and me waving goodbye to our son someday.

After all my dad and Marla have endured together,

they're still going strong. Merging two families, their oldest sons hating one another at first, cancer, grandkids, older parents. They make it look flawless.

Of course I'm ready to ask Clara to marry me. I want my forever to be with her. I just hope she feels the same way.

Chapter Twenty-six

Clara

Friday comes so fast. I can't believe we're about to go public to the world. We're fortunate that after the season ends, no one really cares who Xavier Greene is dating. Well, some might, but everyone is more interested in him during the season than off-season. We've had an easy go so far, but I know that Xavier is worried about backlash and what the mean girls will say.

I've already dealt with them by just being his friend. The eye rolls, the appraisals up and down my body, the judgment on how I'm dressed or how can I only be friends with Xavier Greene, I must be sleeping with him.

None of it truly bothers me. I loved Xavier as a friend and now as a boyfriend. No one else has to understand that, only the two of us. Did Giulia make me self-conscious? Of course. She was one of those one percent of people who look perfect. She was the most beautiful woman I've ever seen up close.

Xavier comes into his great room wearing jeans and an ivory sweater. "Boy, don't we look like Alaska."

I look down at my jeans, sweater that hits my waist, and fuzzy socks. "I'll take my socks off." I sit on the couch.

"No, you won't. Your feet will freeze and turn blue."

"I can at least put on socks that aren't so puffy."

"Clara, stop it. I want you the way you are. I love you and your cozy socks, except when we're in bed." He laughs and sits next to me. "I always get so jittery before these things. I can cancel. Do you want to cancel?"

"No. We're going to do it."

"Fine," he says like a toddler who's been told he has to eat his vegetables.

The doorbell rings and my stomach somersaults. This is it.

Xavier stands. "They'll have to get set up, so you have a bit of time if you want to go take a shot of vodka or something."

"That does sound appealing." I smile, and he smiles back.

Once he's out of view, I breathe a few times to get rid of the anxiety plaguing me. I hear the exchange of hellos. For some reason, I was expecting a woman, not a man. The closer their voices get, the more the nerves set in. I want to do a good job of this for X. Before I can do another breathing exercise, Xavier walks into the room with a guy behind him, and a camera guy, and a woman with a notepad.

"This is Clara," Xavier says, and I stand. He comes next to me, putting his arm around my waist and pulling me flush against him as if he's King Kong ready to climb the Empire State Building. "Clara, this is Mark, Paul, and Millie."

They each wave.

Mark, who was leading the pack and is wearing a suit, steps up, and I assume he's the interviewer. "Mark Roper."

I shake his hand.

"Don't worry about the camera, it's just here to get anything I miss. And Millie takes notes just in case. So when

I'm writing the article, I don't forget anything. Like whether you look uncomfortable when I ask you those tough questions." He laughs and his stained yellow teeth come into view, setting off a creepy vibe.

He's just a guy here to interview you. Relax, Clara.

Mark points at the couch. "Is this where you two are most comfortable?"

Xavier looks around. "Yeah."

"And I have in my notes that we'll do a little tour of your small town too."

"It's adorable. We stayed at the Sunbay Inn last night," Millie says.

"Oh." I look at Xavier, and he shakes his head ever so slightly.

"What?" Millie asks, head tilted.

"They have a great chef," I say, since I'm assuming Xavier doesn't want me to say that Mandi is his stepsister.

"Oh, I ate breakfast there, but last night we went to the local brewery," Millie says. She's all smiles and I feel like we could be friends. Why is Xavier being so grumpy?

"That's his brothers' place," I say, and Xavier's fingers dig into my hip.

"A cute brunette helped us," Mark chimes in. "She had some ass on her."

My body stiffens and Xavier runs his hand down my hip.

"That would be my stepbrother's girlfriend. She's pregnant with his kid." A coldness enters the room from Xavier's voice.

"Oh, congrats to him. If I'd known there were this many good-looking women in small towns, I wouldn't be wasting my time in New York."

Millie rolls her eyes.

"Would you guys like a drink?" I slide out of Xavier's

arm, and I swear he reaches for me. "We have water, soda, coffee, tea?"

"I'd love a water," Mark says.

"What about you, Paul? Millie?" I look between them.

"I'll come help you," Millie says.

Millie joins me in the kitchen, and I grab some bottles of water and the carafe I put the coffee in, along with some cups. "It's winter in Alaska. You always need something warm to offer guests."

"It's going to warm up soon though, right?" she asks.

We both look out the window at the snow-covered ground.

"Soon," I say, then we laugh. "Where are you from?"

"Canada originally, but I moved to New York for a job and well, here I am."

"It must be fun to interview so many celebrities and sports personalities." I place everything we need on a tray to take out to the great room.

"I love my job, not necessarily who I work with." She eyes Mark in the great room, and I'm pretty sure I know why. "Actually, I was wondering... I don't want to be nosy, I swear, but isn't Logan Stone married to someone from this town?"

"Um..."

"It's just that I interviewed him a few years ago and I heard he's got a baby now and is happily married. He kind of gave me my first break. Thought I'd thank him."

I look over at Xavier, whose hand is on the back of his neck as if he's stressed out. "He's actually married to Xavier's stepsister. He owns a gym in town. I can see if I can set up a meeting time if you'd like."

Her face lights up. "I'd love that."

"Millie, I'm sure they don't want us to be here all day," Mark says with some bite in his tone.

"We can talk after?" she says in a low voice.

"Sure." I smile.

Xavier looks at the tray I prepared when I rejoin them, and Mark takes a water, cracking it open. "If you're ready, we can start any time."

"Shoot," Xavier says, and I lean back on the couch under his extended arm.

Mark begins by asking us to explain how we grew up, how Xavier made it all the way to playing football professionally, and once we're done with all that, he starts in with the questions about our relationship.

"So, you made a vague comment about finding love a few months ago, but mentioned that you were keeping the mystery woman a secret?"

Xavier nods. "Yeah. We were just starting out and I didn't want to put any pressure on either of us."

Mark smiles at me. "A lot of people assumed you meant Sessilee Adams, Giulia, your ex's best friend."

"No, that was actually a double date I went on. That's the only time I've had dinner with Sessilee, although she's a nice woman." Xavier's body is so filled with tension I fear he's going to crack apart next to me.

"I'm sure it's no surprise to either of you that most people assumed the woman in question was a model or an actress. Someone else in the limelight."

Xavier inhales deeply, but just by looking at him, you'd never guess how on edge he is. He's always been able to mask that. To everyone but me. I place my hand on his knee, hoping to relax him.

"I'm not sure why they'd assume that," he says.

"Well, you're Xavier Greene. You signed the biggest deal of any quarterback in the league. Your history is dating models."

"One. I dated one model."

Mark blinks rapidly at the coolness of Xavier's tone. "All right, let's move on. Clara Harrison, the small-town librarian. It's almost right out of a romantic comedy movie." Mark smiles at me, but I no longer like him, so I give a tight smile in return.

"You could say that," Xavier says.

"Xavier told me you've been best friends since kindergarten?" Mark says.

"Yes." I nod.

"And all those years, the two of you never crossed the line from friendship to something more?"

"No," Xavier answers quickly. "We were best friends, and now she's my girlfriend."

Mark laughs. "Okay. Okay. But the road to finding one another... looking at each other in a different light... that's what people want to hear about."

I sit up straighter, ready to take charge of the interview since Xavier isn't having any of it. "It was just one night that made the difference. Xavier got a little jealous about the attention I was getting from another man, and I guess things spiraled from there." I squeeze X's knee.

"Spiraled how? And Xavier Greene jealous of another man?"

Millie is typing on her computer next to Mark, and Paul has the camera on us.

"Should Xavier not get jealous?" The question falls out of my mouth, and I know I was snippier than I intended when I see Mark's face.

"Well, again, no offense, Clara, but he's Xavier Greene. He could easily move on to another woman."

Xavier sits up, his arm out from around my shoulders.

"Not when the woman I want is with someone else. Clara is the one I want."

"Of course she is. She's cute as a button in those fluffy socks."

I want to hide my feet. Millie frowns and glares at Mark.

"Next question," Xavier says.

Thankfully, Mark gets off the topic of me and talks about Xavier's season a bit. Then he hits us with the question I can tell he's been holding back until the end. "So, you obviously can't play football living in Sunrise Bay, and you can't be a librarian in San Francisco. At least not in a small-town library like the one you run now. What does that mean for your relationship next year? Will you be breaking the hearts of San Francisco women and relocating with Xavier for the season?"

"We haven't figured out all the details yet," I say. "I'm sure we will before the season starts."

Xavier narrows his eyes at me but says nothing.

Mark asks a few basic follow-up questions and then stands. "All right, let's go get a tour of this small town."

Paul turns off the camera.

"I'll be right back," Xavier says and goes upstairs without another word.

I take the tray back to the kitchen while Millie, Mark, and Paul get packed up, but I hear Mark talking to Paul.

"Poor girl. She'll be his during this off-season, but mark my words, by next year, Xavier will have another model on his arm. Don't get me wrong, the girl is pretty for the girl-next-door type, but the best quarterback in the league doesn't date an average girl. Eventually, their different lifestyles will get to them, and he'll break her heart. This town will hate him for it, and he'll never return. Seen this scenario a dozen times. Funny though, why do men have these unresolved feelings for the girls of their past? It's so cliché, it's pathetic really. And the girl won't even see it coming. She'll be living in some bubble where she's playing house while he's getting his dick sucked by someone else."

Paul doesn't say much and exits the house with his camera. Mark follows, but when I come out of the kitchen, Millie is nowhere to be found.

Xavier comes down with his parka on and a hat, looking as pissed off as ever.

"What's wrong?"

"I'm going to punch that guy in the face. After he leaves, I'm calling my agent. That asshole isn't getting a story on me. Not when he made all those condescending remarks to you."

"Well, he's a reporter. He's supposed to try to get a rise out of us," I say, excusing his behavior even after all the shit I overheard him telling the camera guy. I just wish time would fast forward so I can prove him wrong. Xavier and I are going to make it.

"You stay here. I'm telling them we're not going through town and that he can go fuck himself. I'm not gonna listen to him be disrespectful to you any more than I already have today."

"Xavier," I sigh, but who am I to stop him? Mark *is* an asshole.

Millie comes out of the bathroom.

"I'll text Logan right now and ask him to meet you at The Grind," I say.

"Thanks so much, and I'm really sorry about Mark. He's a jackass. I think you and Xavier make a very cute couple. A real-life couple." She smiles.

"Thank you, Millie."

She walks out, and as the door opens, I hear Xavier tell

Mark, "You think you can talk to her like that? You release one word of this interview and I'm suing your ass."

I can't hear what Mark says, but Xavier returns a few minutes later, slamming the door.

So much for a casual interview about finding love while playing the game.

Chapter Twenty-seven

Clara

Two weeks after the interview, the weather is finally getting a little warmer and the ground is beginning to thaw.

Xavier is in his lower level working out when there's a knock on the door.

I open it to find Presley and Leighton.

"I went by your place and you weren't there so I figured I'd find you here. Do you live here now?" she asks.

"Kind of, but we're still very much back and forth."

She walks in, hands me Leighton, then drops the diaper bag on the floor. "You're officially on aunt duty. My arms hurt." She heads into the kitchen and opens the freezer before swearing and slamming it shut.

"Um, Pres, what's going on?"

"I'm a horrible person. A horrible mother. A horrible wife." She breaks down in a fit of tears, burying her head in her hands.

My chest tightens. What the hell is going on?

Leighton smiles at me as though she doesn't have a care in the world.

"No, you're not. Tell me what's going on?"

She peeks through her fingers and says, "I'm pregnant." It's all muffled, but the words are clear as day.

My eyes widen. "Seriously?"

She nods. "And I'm about ready to die. Do you realize Leighton just started sleeping through the night? I've had one month of bliss, and I haven't even lost all my baby weight yet."

I grab the diaper bag and pull out a few toys for Leighton. I build a little fort with the abundance of throw pillows Xavier owns and toss a few toys in there. She happily sits up and digs through the little toys. Turning on the television, I put on a kids' channel to keep her entertained then walk over to my sister.

"It's going to be fine." I rub her back.

"I might as well turn into a zombie. The bookstore is hardly even open because of how much I take off with Leighton. How will I ever manage with two?"

I put my arm around her and guide her to the couch.

The treadmill stops downstairs, and I hear Xavier coming up the steps. He stops at the top of the stairs and looks at Presley. "Did someone die?"

"No," I answer.

"Did Cade leave town?"

Presley glares at him.

I shake my head. "No."

"Someone sick?"

"No."

"Can I tell him?" I ask Presley.

"No," she says. "Not until..."

I shake my head and point upstairs. Xavier blows out a breath but goes upstairs without another word. I hear the television click on before he shuts the door and turns on the shower.

"Okay, first thing is you have to tell Cade. I mean, he is the father, right?"

She rolls her eyes. "Funny, Clara. Yes, he's the father."

"Why don't you go into Xavier's office and call him? Ask him to come over, and the two of you go for a walk. We'll watch Leighton."

She nods but doesn't move.

I tap her shoulder. "This is where you get up and walk."

"I'm scared. I mean, we never talked about it. When we'd want another. I'm on the minipill. But there was this one night when we didn't have a lot of time and we were out of condoms and thought what are the chances…" She points at her stomach. "Pretty damn good apparently. I should play the lottery."

"Just go call him. You guys can handle two. I'll help out more."

She groans and gets up, walking to Xavier's office.

I sit down next to Leighton, pick up her stuffed giraffe, and prance it around the pillows, making her laugh. I hear the bedroom door swing open upstairs.

"I'm gonna kill the bastard." Xavier rushes down the stairs.

"There are impressionable little ears down here." I point at Leighton.

"You're never going to believe this. That Mark guy wrote a nasty article about me. Said how he came all the way to Alaska to interview me about my love life and I was rude to him. That you were like a housewife from the fifties, ready to fetch my paper, prepare my eggs, and alluded to giving me blow jobs on request. He said I kicked him off my property."

"Well, you kind of did do that," I say.

"After he was an asshole to you. He called Sunrise Bay a Podunk town and you just some small-town girl who probably doesn't realize how famous I am."

I want to confess to Xavier what I heard the guy say about me, but I don't want to upset him any more than he already is.

"Oh, and he said how we'd live separate lives next year because we probably have some open relationship where I can screw whoever I want while you wait at home for me to return. What kinda sick shit is this?" Xavier flops down on the couch, face red and his hands in fists.

The office door opens.

"Hey, Clara," Presley says. "Your computer was charging in there. You got an email, and I was snooping." She shrugs and hands me my computer.

I get up, take a seat on the couch beside Xavier, and position the laptop on my lap.

"Want to tell me what the tears are for?" Xavier asks Presley. "I can still kick my brother's ass if need be."

"He's on his way over. We just need to talk over some things."

Xavier studies her for a beat then nods tersely.

It's from an email I don't recognize, sent to my library email address. "This is weird."

"Who's it from?" Xavier leans over my shoulder.

"I'm not sure."

I press *Play* and it's a video of when Mark talked shit about me to Paul.

"What the fuck?" Xavier takes the computer from me. His knuckles turn white from tightening around my computer, his nostrils flaring. "Why would they send this to you? Who is this?"

I hold up my hands. "I don't know."

He puts the computer on the coffee table and paces the room, pushing his hands through his hair.

"What's going on?" Presley comes to my side, and I press *Play* on the video again while reading the email.

I HATE TO DO THIS, but I want you to be prepared because I'm going to post it online. What he did to Xavier today is crap and it's time everyone knows what kind of person Mark is. Sorry I filmed this without you knowing, but I'm Team Clara. ~ Millie

"OH, IT'S FROM MILLIE," I say, and Xavier comes and sits next to me. "She's posting it online. I could tell she was fed up with Mark, but this is crazy. First Mark writes that article—"

"I'd rather people think I'm an asshole than have this video out there that's bashing you," Xavier says.

"I have to agree with Xavier on this," Presley says. "I mean, this man is just mean. Where is he from? New York? I have connections."

We both turn to look at her. "What kind of connections? Rich girls who can poke his eye out with their stilettos?" I say and wink so she knows I'm kidding.

In response, she sticks her tongue out at me.

I put the computer back on the table and pace myself. Leighton follows me with her eyes, her little neck circling around. The door opens and Cade walks in.

"Ever heard of knocking?" Xavier says.

"You're my little brother. I'm never knocking." He heads right over to Presley. "What's going on? I'm worried."

She shoos him with her hand. "It can wait. I need you to charter a plane to New York so I can kick this guy's ass." She points at the computer screen.

Cade sits down next to his wife and watches the video, then turns to Xavier. "And you're still here?"

"Believe me, I'm mentally preparing a guys' trip to New York tonight. Just figuring out how we can get in and out of town with an alibi."

"Perfect." Cade nods.

"And one woman!" Presley raises her hand. "Clara can watch Leighton."

"Stop it, all of you! This is my fight." I glare at them with my hands on my hips.

"Like hell it is," Xavier says and crosses the room to me. "I'm your boyfriend."

I rest my hand on his bicep. "You guys need to calm down. You don't need any more bad press. I can handle this."

Xavier grabs my hand. "I need to talk to you for a second." We go to his office, and he shuts the door. "Did you hear him when he said those things?"

I sigh. "I did."

"Figured. You let him speak that way about you in my house and didn't tell me? Thank fuck I kicked him out, but we're a team, Clara."

I stare at him for a beat. "I know that, but you didn't need to hear it. You were already upset, and I don't care what that guy thinks of me. His opinion of me does not matter."

"I'm glad you feel that way, but I want us to conquer these things together."

I chuckle and shake my head.

"What?"

"You want me to tell you this type of thing so you can handle it for us. Just like the library extension, that was very Team Xavier and Clara."

He frowns. "That's different."

"Is it?" I raise my eyebrows.

"I said I was sorry."

"And I forgave you, but this is my fight, not yours. But I will let you know what happens when I decide what to do. I want to know one thing."

He waits for me to continue. Now that we're just putting it all out there, I might as well ask the question that's been nagging me for a while.

"Do you expect me to follow you to San Francisco and not work anymore? Or even when you're off-season, to not be a librarian?"

"Yeah, I thought something was on your mind." He wraps his arms around my waist. "You're kind of transparent when you're stewing over something. I want you to do whatever you want. But the option is there if you don't want to work. I'm more than happy to take care of you."

"I want to work," I assure him.

"Okay." He kisses my forehead. "Now, I'm going to be gone a day or so." He unhooks himself from me and starts to walk away, but I grab his arm, pulling him back.

"Please just give me a chance to handle this first. If my way fails, then you can go to New York and do whatever you want."

He stares at me for a long moment then nods. "This goes against everything I was taught when I was a kid."

"I know. Just give me an hour."

"And you want me to go out there?" He thumbs in the direction of the door.

"Yep."

"You owe me." He kisses my forehead one more time and steps away from me. "No clown outfit for you."

He opens the door and leaves, shutting it behind him.

I sit at Xavier's desk and use his computer. I start typing

a letter, hoping that fighting words with words is the best solution for this situation.

For an hour, I type, delete, and type again. I release all of my feelings on that page and hope it's received well. Then I send it to a few news stations, including TMZ. I send it to Nikki, who I know can get it in the right hands, asking her to distribute it as she sees fit. And I tag Mark in every post I make.

Then I sit back and wait to see what happens now that the pin is out of the grenade.

Chapter Twenty-eight

"I guess that means I have your family's blessing."
— Xavier

Xavier

Clara is still in the office when I receive a text message from Ben.

You really are a lucky bastard.

There's a link attached that I click on, and an article pops up.

The real life of the star quarterback's best friend.

"Shit, guys. Clara wrote her own reply." I copy and paste the link to both Cade and Presley's emails.

Then I read the article.

Other than his family, I've known Xavier Greene the longest in his life. We were only in kindergarten when our friendship started. Two innocent little kids. He loved playing football because his older brothers played, and I loved to play house. We had nothing in common, yet we always gravitated toward one another. We were both teased, and many didn't believe we could only be platonic friends.

To many in this world, he is Xavier Greene, Kingsmen starting quarterback. The hot football player who got the big contract. The man who's dated one of the most beautiful women in the world. But to me...

He's the first boy I loved.

He's my first crush.

He's my first kiss.

He's my first dance partner.

He's the one who kept me standing while I watched my mom's body lowered into the ground.

He's the one who stayed with me for weeks afterward until I could function.

He's the one constant in my life.

Some people will look at me the same way Mark Roper did and only see a small-town librarian. A girl who never fled from her hometown to gain some real-life experience. A girl who enjoys reading, eating sweets, and watching her best friend play the game he loves. A girl on the sidelines. It's a simple life to most.

My best friend pleaded with me to join him in San Francisco years ago, and I declined that invitation because I'm not a big city girl. I was made for small-town living. I like knowing my neighbors and being part of a community. So judge if you will, but what I always find funny is that most of you are just like me. Most of you won't ever grace the pages of a magazine, or play professional sports, or have a celebrity makeup artist and stylist. But why should one of us not get the chance to be with someone like Xavier? After all, I've been his first kiss, his first dance partner, and I held his hand when his mom died too. Our lives are so intertwined not even Mark and his cynical words can unravel them.

So yeah, I'm not a model, but I am worthy and I'm comfortable with that because my best friend, boyfriend, and lover looks at me like I'm his entire world.

I stand from the couch and head to my office.

"We're gonna go," Cade says.

"Sure thing. Congrats." I wave.

"Congrats for what?" Cade asks Presley.

"I was just starting to like you!" Presley calls.

"Presley?" Cade asks as I open the office door. I don't hear Presley's response, but he shouts, "Shut up! That's awesome!"

Clara is sitting on the floor with her legs crossed, biting her nails. "So? Did Presley tell Cade something?"

"That she's pregnant? Yeah. I sort of forced her into it." I cringe and sit on the floor with her.

"How did you know?"

"Because why else would she be so distraught and not go straight to my brother? Plus, I see her sleep deprivation. It wouldn't be ideal right now. But she'll be happy."

"Yeah."

"I don't want to talk about Cade and Presley. I want to talk about how undeserving I am of you." I take her head in my hands. "It was awesome. I was so stupid for underestimating you. To think you couldn't handle yourself. Of course you could."

"I've had years of practice. Maybe not at the national press level, but I don't care what they say about me. All I care about is what this town thinks of me and, most importantly, how you see me."

"Will you marry me?" The words pour out of me.

"What?" Her face pales and her eyes well up with tears.

"Jesus, I don't have a ring, but marry me, Clara. I want you to be my wife, and I want to be your husband. I want to have a zillion kids with you. I don't want to waste any more time than we already have."

She laughs. "A zillion?"

"Well… after seeing Presley, maybe three?"

"Xavier, are you sure?"

I bring her forward so she's straddling me. "I've never been surer of anything in my life. You are my forever." She hugs me tightly, and I close my eyes, "I'm sorry it's not the proposal you deserve."

"It's okay, X, I don't care about any of that. All I care about is us. I love you. Of course, I'll marry you."

"I love you. Always have, always will." I smash my lips to hers, then I lower her to the floor to make love to my fiancée. Nothing sounds better than that. Except maybe wife.

Two weeks later…

The outpouring of love for Clara was like nothing I've ever seen before. So many go girls, you're worthy, you're deserving, damn right. Mark was fired from the magazine for his unprofessionalism, and the article about me has been taken down and retracted, although I'm sure it lives in cyberspace somewhere.

We're getting out of my truck after celebrating my dad being in remission with the family.

"What's this?" Clara asks, seeing in the back seat the box my dad gave me weeks ago.

"Oh, my dad gave it to me. He and Marla said they were saving it for us and that we had to open it together. I forgot it was in the back seat."

She looks suspicious and takes it with her, along with the leftovers Marla demanded we take.

"So, what do you want to do about next year?" I ask as we approach the house.

"I can't move to San Francisco, but I can come most weekends."

I'm only staying for two more years. Once my contract is up, I'm done. I've made more than I ever thought I would, and if I can retire without injury, I'm happy. Sunrise Bay is where I want to raise our kids, so while two years of a few months of long distance isn't ideal, we'll make it work.

"We better work on our FaceTime sex skills though," she says as I unlock the front door. She walks into the house and drops the box on the kitchen counter, her hands poised to open it.

"Hey, we're supposed to do this together."

"Sorry, I can't believe you just left it in there for how many weeks." She shakes her head.

I shrug. "I had a lot on my mind." I kiss her cheek. "Let me put these leftovers in the fridge, then we'll open it."

She goes to the couch and positions the box on her lap.

The light shines on her diamond ring. A five-carat solitaire on a platinum band. She says it's too much, but nothing is too much for her.

"Okay, open." I sit down on the couch beside her.

She pulls out an old VHS tape and looks at me. Then a photo album. Nothing else is in there. She opens the photo album and gasps. "X?"

I look over her shoulder and sit up straighter. The pictures are of us when we were younger. The first day of kindergarten where we're positioned in front of the school together. And every grade after that. Each one is marked with an X and a C with the year written on the back.

She continues to flip the pages and discover more and more pictures of us.

"Look at us." Clara's finger goes down the page of pictures stuck on sticky boards with clear plastic over the top.

I hold up the VHS. "How are we going to watch this?"

"Do we know anyone who has a VHS player?"

"No."

"We need to get one."

I look them up on my phone and find one to buy that will be delivered in two days. "They're more expensive than when they were first out."

She leans back on me with the photo album. "I can't believe they kept all these."

We go through all the pictures and the accompanying memories. It's fun to find out that we each remember some things differently than the other.

I kiss her temple, still unable to believe that we're here. After all this time, we're more than we ever thought we'd be.

TWO DAYS LATER...

"X!" Clara screams down at me. "It's here!"

I turn off the treadmill and rush up the stairs. She's already got the box ripped open and is trying to figure out the cables and things on the back of the television.

"That looks like a nightmare." I wipe my face with my towel.

I help her, and all in all, it takes a half hour to get the VCR hooked up the right way. Once it is, we sit on the floor, pressing *Play*. It starts with static, then Clara comes on screen wearing a white lacy dress. She's maybe seven or eight, I'd guess.

"Come on, Xavier, it's cute."

Clara looks at me because it's my mom's voice. My breath stutters halfway up my throat. It's been so long since I've heard it, but it's like a balm to my soul.

"X?" Little Clara calls to me.

"The boys are gonna make fun of me." I come out of a room dressed in a suit that must've been Cade's because I hadn't grown into it yet.

"No, they're not," my mom says.

Little Clara tells me to stand by the giant gorilla, then she walks down the aisle toward me.

"They're so sweet," Clara's mom says, and the video pans to her for a second where we see tears streaming down her face.

"We have to save this for when they're older. Imagine if they really do get married?" my mom says in the background.

"We'd be related. Have to say, I wouldn't mind spending all the holidays with you." Clara's mom laughs.

"You have to say I do," Little Clara says to Little Xavier.

"I do," I say reluctantly.

We say our vows and hug instead of kiss. Then we run down the aisle and Clara throws her bouquet into the stuffed animal crowd.

"Mommy," Little Clara says. "I married Xavier."

"I saw. But we need to go home for dinner." She rubs Clara's back.

"I go where Xavier goes. He's my husband."

I side-eye my fiancée and laugh. "So Little Clara would've gone to San Francisco with me." She shoves me with her elbow, and I wrap my arm around her shoulders. "Just kidding. It's been so long since I heard her voice."

She wipes her face. "Me too."

At the end of the video, our moms turn the camera to them and we gasp at the same time.

"Xavier and Clara, eight years old." They both have their fingers crossed as if they're hoping we'll end up together.

"I guess that means I have your family's blessing."

She nods. "Want to play it again?"

"Definitely."

We watch the video over and over, in each other's arms.

"Do you think they know we fell in love?" Clara looks up at me.

I nod. "I think they knew then it was inevitable."

She laughs and wiggles in my arms. "Probably." Turning her head to meet my gaze, she says, "I love you."

"And I love you. Although just so we're clear, you forced me to say I do back then."

"Not this time. You can't wait to marry me now."

I grin. "Damn right."

Epilogue

Xavier

*A*fter we found the tape, we realized how fast time goes by and we didn't want to take years to plan a big wedding. So with the help of a lot of people in town, and of course Marla, we pulled off a wedding in only one month.

The first day of spring, I stand in what was my old bedroom, putting on my tuxedo. Clara is a few doors down in Posey's old room. We're getting married in Hank and Marla's backyard.

My dad pokes his head in. "Ready?"

"Yep."

He walks in and hands me the bracelet that was once my mom's. "Marla wants to know if you want to give this to her yourself or have her give it to her as her something old."

"Let me write a note real quick." I find a piece of paper and pen.

THIS IS YOUR SOMETHING OLD. *It was my mom's and I'd be honored if you wore it on our special day. She would have loved to have you as her daughter-in-law. See you at the end of the aisle. Love, X*

· · ·

I HAND it to my dad, and he says he'll be right back.

The next thing I know, we're being told it's time for me to go downstairs. We opted for no groomsmen or bridesmaids, just the two of us. In a family as big as ours, a wedding party can get out of control real fast. We did ask Emelia to be the flower girl and Trey, Adam and Lucy's now adopted son, to be the ring bearer though.

I head down the stairs and out back. Although it's spring, it's not that warm out. Doesn't matter. My only goals for today are to make Clara my wife and make sure she enjoys our day.

I give a nod to Ben, Ashton, and a few other teammates I invited. It's a small wedding and decorated moderately. I chuckle, thinking the Xavier from a couple years ago would be disappointed that *People* magazine wasn't here doing an exclusive story. What an idiot I was.

The music begins shortly after I arrive at the end of the aisle, and Clara walks out of the back door on my dad's arm. Her white dress clings to her small curves. She has subtle makeup and no veil. She looks perfect.

She walks past the white chairs with our guests, smiling at everyone, her white flower bouquet gripped tightly in her hand. By the time she reaches me, I'm already antsy since the women in our family insisted we had to spend last night apart. I feel as if I haven't gotten to look at Clara in months, and my eyes soak her in.

"Hi," she says after my dad shakes my hand and kisses her cheek before sitting down.

"You look stunning."

Her cheeks pinken. "Thank you. You look so handsome."

"You should see what I'm wearing underneath." I wink and she laughs.

The officiant clears his throat and we both straighten up to pay attention.

We say our vows and exchange rings, and when the officiant tells us we can kiss, I dip her, kissing her sweetly.

We make our way down the aisle, smiling at all of the important people in our lives and go into the house to take a few moments to ourselves.

"I'm Mrs. Xavier Greene. Mrs. Greene. Clara Greene. Are you sure you don't want to be Harrison?"

"Yeah, I'm pretty sure." I chuckle.

We take a moment to really kiss one another, then stand there holding each other and savoring the moment.

Ben shouts into the house, "Come on, it's time to party!"

We come out to join everyone. Sure enough, the yard has already been transformed into a party. A DJ who played the music for the ceremony puts on colored lights now and the music is pumping. Propane heaters are strategically placed to keep the nip out of the air, and the only two people on the dance floor are Cam and Chevelle. Fisher, Cade, and Adam are on the outskirts, watching them with their arms crossed.

I feel pulled to join them.

Mandi is at a table, lost in her phone.

"Time for the bride and groom to have their first dance," the DJ says.

I lead Clara out to the dance floor, and as I spin her around the first time, the projection screen comes down and the video of us getting married at eight years old plays.

Our family members gush over the video, not having seen it before, and my dad and Marla watch Clara and me with smiles on their faces and tears in their eyes. Some of my family are in tears, some are in disbelief, but mostly I see smiles. I have no doubt that all the people we love who have already passed on are all here tonight, smiling down on us.

I take my wife in my arms and slowly move us around the dance floor. Our foreheads resting on one another's, we stare into each other's eyes.

"Still scared?" she asks.

"No. I'm just happy as hell you waited for me."

"Always."

WE ARRIVE HOME from our honeymoon in Bali to a big pile of mail at both of our houses.

When we get to my house, we decide to go through the stack while we relax on the couch.

"So much junk mail," Clara says. "Should we tell the family we're home?"

"No. We have at least one more night without them knowing." I bring her a drink and sit down next to her.

"This one looks interesting." She flips around a gray envelope. "No return address, but it's addressed to Mr. and Mrs. Greene. Our first piece of couple mail." She holds it to her heart and bats her eyelashes.

"Huh," I say. "Open it."

She carefully tears it open as though she's going to frame it or something. Her eyes widen when she sees what's inside. "Um, did we miss a message string while we were gone?"

I frown. "Why?"

She holds up what looks like an invitation. "Mandi is getting married? To Noah, Midge's grandson?"

I tear the piece of paper out of her hand and read it for myself.

She reaches for her phone on the coffee table. I grab it before she gets it.

"X!"

"No. One more night, then we'll find out what it's all about. Just me and you for one more night, okay?"

She lets out a breath. "You owe me."

"Fine, I'll wear the clown underwear."

She smiles. "Deal. I'll wait until tomorrow, but man, I'm in shock."

"The grandmas really worked their magic quick on those two."

"Isn't that the truth."

We both laugh, knowing Mandi's in for it.

The End

ALSO BY PIPER RAYNE

The Baileys

Lessons from a One-Night Stand (FREE)

Advice from a Jilted Bride

Birth of a Baby Daddy

Operation Bailey Wedding (Novella)

Falling for My Brother's Best Friend

Demise of a Self-Centered Playboy

Confessions of a Naughty Nanny

Operation Bailey Babies (Novella)

Secrets of the World's Worst Matchmaker

Winning my Best Friend's Girl

Rules for Dating Your Ex

Operation Bailey Birthday (Novella)

The Greene Family

My Twist of Fortune (Free Prequel)

My Beautiful Neighbor (FREE)

My Almost Ex

My Vegas Groom

A Greene Family Summer Bash (Novella)

My Sister's Flirty Friend

My Unexpected Surprise

My Famous Frenemy

A Greene Family Vacation (Novella)

My Scorned Best Friend

My Fake Fiancé

My Brother's Forbidden Friend

A Greene Family Christmas (Novella)

Lake Starlight

The Problem with Second Chances

The Issue with Bad Boy Roommates

The Trouble with Runaway Brides

The Drawback of Single Dads

Plain Daisy Ranch

One Last Summer

The One I Left Behind

The One I Stood Beside

The One I Didn't See Coming

Modern Love

Charmed by the Bartender

Hooked by the Boxer

Mad about the Banker

Single Dads Club

Real Deal

Dirty Talker

Sexy Beast

Hollywood Hearts

Mister Mom

Animal Attraction

Domestic Bliss

Bedroom Games

Cold as Ice

On Thin Ice

Break the Ice

Chicago Law

Smitten with the Best Man

Tempted by my Ex-Husband

Seduced by my Ex's Divorce Attorney

Blue Collar Brothers

Flirting with Fire

Crushing on the Cop

Engaged to the EMT

White Collar Brothers

Sexy Filthy Boss

Dirty Flirty Enemy

Wild Steamy Hook-up

The Rooftop Crew

My Bestie's Ex

A Royal Mistake

The Rival Roomies

Our Star-Crossed Kiss

The Do-Over

A Co-Workers Crush

Hockey Hotties

Countdown to a Kiss (Free Prequel)

My Lucky #13 (FREE)

The Trouble with #9

Faking it with #41

Tropical Hat Trick (Novella)

Sneaking around with #34

Second Shot with #76

Offside with #55

Kingsmen Football Stars

False Start (Free Prequel)

You Had Your Chance, Lee Burrows

You Can't Kiss the Nanny, Brady Banks

Over My Brother's Dead Body, Chase Andrews

Chicago Grizzlies

On the Defense (Free Prequel)

Something like Hate

Something like Lust

Something like Love

The Nest

Mr. Heartbreaker

Mr. Broody

Mr. S (Title to be revealed)

Mr. C (Title to be revealed)

Holiday Romances

Single and Ready to Jingle

Claus and Effect

Merry Kissmas

Cockamamie Unicorn Ramblings

Xavier and Clara... their story was supposed to be book nine in the series but we bumped it up to book seven because we knew that was way too long of a time for them to not be speaking to one another or discover that there were more to their feelings than friendship.

When we were plotting out the series, we knew early on that they would cross the line which would cause their friendship to take a fork in the road. Way back when we weren't exactly sure WHAT their parting ways would be about, but it's called My Scorned Best Friend so there had to have been a fight. LOL And we had the idea of Clara no longer writing his number on her cheek and being interested in his football games while no one else would really know what went down.

We usually start really nailing down storylines a couple books before so we can weave more details in. So when we were at the tail end of Posey's book we decided we wanted to up the stakes by having one of Xavier's friends want to date Clara. Enter Ben Noughton who came on page during the My Famous Frenemy bonus scene. We really love Ben and hope he finds his happily ever after. ;)

We always say that no book goes according to plan, and there were some new things that came about in this one that we didn't originally plan for. The video tape of them when they were younger came up during writing, but we felt as if they needed something with both of their mom's blessing to really close the loop on both their losses. We spent way more time in San Francisco then we thought we would. And although we love Ben, he just wouldn't leave the damn story.

As always, we have a lot of people to thank for getting this book into your hands...

Nina and the entire Valentine PR team.
Cassie from Joy Editing for line edits.
Ellie from My Brother's Editor for line edits.
Rosa from My Brother's Editor for proofreading.
Hang Le for the cover and branding for the entire series.
Wander Aguiar for his awesome job of giving us our muses Xavier and Clara.
Bloggers who consistently carve out time to read, review and/or promote us.
Piper Rayne Unicorns who are the best readers out there!
Readers who took the time to read our story when there's so many choices out there. We are grateful beyond words for your support!

You know we love leaving you with cliffhangers for the next book. What do you think happened? How is Mandi already engaged to Noah? There's a lot to their story that might surprise you.

xo,
Piper & Rayne

ABOUT PIPER & RAYNE

Piper Rayne is a USA Today Bestselling Author duo who write "heartwarming humor with a side of sizzle" about families, whether that be blood or found. They both have e-readers full of one-clickable books, they're married to husbands who drive them to drink, and they're both chauffeurs to their kids. Most of all, they love hot heroes and quirky heroines who make them laugh, and they hope you do, too!